TALKS LIKE THUNDER

RED WITH NATIVE BLOOD

BOOK ONE

MARJORIE CARTER

RANDAL NERHUS

SOUL MISSION PUBLICATIONS

INTRODUCTION

For the whole of my life, I have been drawn to Indian history, much the same as a grizzly is to a honey-filled tree. And like him, I have often suffered the stinging. It has been a small price to pay for the sweet knowledge of the ancients and the days of long ago.

One of the gifts of my heritage is seeing. Almost every tribe had a seer, a person with the ability to see the past as well as the future. While exploring mountainous terrain in western New Mexico, I was struck by a vision from the past. So vivid was the vision that I could not only see the battle in detail, but I could also smell the smoke and feel the pain of the dying people.

I attempted to identify the exact time and place of the battle; however, so many massacres took place in this period of our history that I cannot say with any degree of accuracy which particular battle I saw. Therefore, my story is fiction, and the characters are based upon my interpretation of the vision.

Marjorie Carter, Rancho Los Lobos, Corralejo, Mexico, 2004

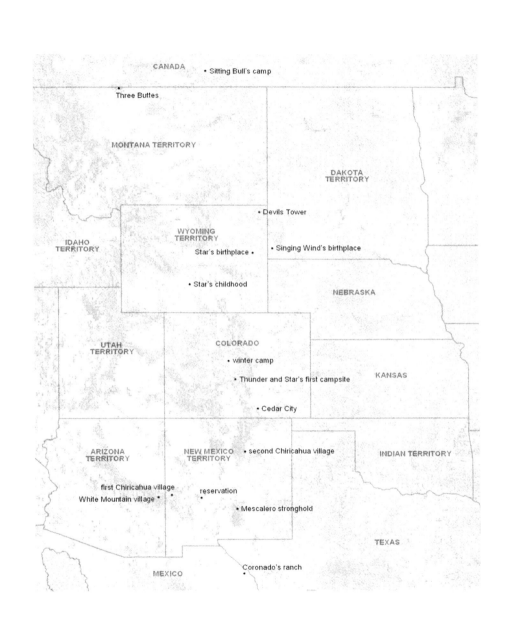

CANADA • Sitting Bull's camp

• Three Buttes

MONTANA TERRITORY

DAKOTA
TERRITORY

• Devils Tower

WYOMING
TERRITORY

IDAHO
TERRITORY

Star's birthplace •   • Singing Wind's birthplace

NEBRASKA

• Star's childhood

UTAH
TERRITORY

COLORADO

• winter camp

• Thunder and Star's first campsite   KANSAS

• Cedar City

ARIZONA
TERRITORY

NEW MEXICO
TERRITORY   • second Chiricahua village   INDIAN TERRITORY

first Chiricahua village •   • reservation

White Mountain village •

• Mescalero stronghold

TEXAS

MEXICO   • Coronado's ranch

TALKS LIKE THUNDER

While walking Bear Claw Mountain
A strange thing I did see.
The sun fell down, the sky turned black
And a vision came to me.

Cold winds howled; the heavens parted
Mother Earth stood perfectly still.
A ghastly scene appeared before me
Of a village on a hill.

Its beautiful painted tipis
Crushed and lying in the mud.
The snow was white no more
But red with native blood.

Young sons and warriors running
Singing, "It is a good day to die."
They could not stop the enemy
Yet they gave their lives to try.

A young girl raped and screaming
When a knife sliced through the air.
A soldier bent, then walked away
His badge of courage was her hair.

A mother raced across the field
Pleading, "Do not kill my son."
She fell too like all the rest
Head smashed by a soldier's gun.

Saw her newborn baby's body
With a bayonet through his chest.
Saw how he jerked, then shuddered
When he drew his final breath.

Smelled the smoke and saw the burning
And the cavalry ride away.
Heard the gaiety of their laughter
For a victory shared that day.

Saw a girl of fifteen winters
When she climbed atop the knoll.
Heard her anguished cry of mourning
The sound still echoes in my soul.

—Marjorie Carter

ONE

Arizona Territory, June 1871

As Desert Flower sank the clay pot into the glistening stream, she lost her grip, and the current carried it away. She ran around a patch of sweet grass, planted her foot into the stream, reached out, and grabbed it. She tried filling the pot one-handed, as she always had, but it wobbled around, refusing to tip. *Why is this thing so hard to fill? I would hate to get my bracelet wet.* The pot continued to move and bob until she finally gave up, and plunged it down with both hands. Something about the water bubbling and gurgling seemed like a kind of forewarning. Dismissing the thought, she heaved the heavy pot onto her hip, consoling herself that it was just too big for her. The aroma of the blooming sweet grass, like the smell after a rain, made her smile. She strode up the bare stone path, ignoring her cramping stomach, and returned to her White Mountain Apache village. Happy that her people shared their food and provided shelter, she knew that even without parents, it was home.

The rumble of horses driven hard ruptured Desert Flower's musings. A growing line of dust swirling above the treetops raced toward the village. Thirteen warriors swept into sight, heavily armed and painted for war. As they penetrated the settlement and halted their horses, dust filtered across the wikiups made of grass and brush. The riders gazed upon the villagers—their red and black faces so ferocious, no one dared look them in the eyes.

The oldest warrior sat astride a huge white stallion painted with yellow marks of lightning. Bold red zigzags adorned the man's weathered face, and large silver hoops dangled from his ears. A turquoise-studded eagle-bone breastplate draped over his fine deer-skin shirt, and wind tossed his thick, black hair about his shoulders. Tiny silver bells, interwoven into the long fringe hanging from his sleeves, tinkled as he moved.

Desert Flower gaped in wonder at the old man. Never in her seven winters had she seen such an astonishing show of wealth.

A riderless stallion pranced beside the old man. Its sleek black body shimmered in the bright sunlight, and its long, tapered legs moved like those of an elegant dancer.

The man dismounted in a whirlwind of grace and color, and hushed murmurs rippled through the crowd. He stabbed his lance into the ground with such force, its snake rattles clattered and its eagle feathers danced. Facing the villagers, he declared, "I am Gray Fox, *nantan* of the Three Hills Chiricahua Apaches. I learned in a dream two sleeps ago that the life force of she who was my daughter-in-law has departed. I have come to claim the child belonging to her and to he who was my son."

Desert Flower shuddered in terror. The pot slid from her hip, hit the bare stone, and shattered.

Gray Fox surveyed the onlookers. "Where is your *nantan*?"

A village boy threw back the hide covering the entrance to Chief White Cloud's home. Gray Fox strode powerfully toward the lodge and disappeared inside. The Chiricahua warriors remained mounted —their dark, brooding eyes never leaving the crowd for an instant.

As Desert Flower ran toward White Cloud's lodge, a memory came to her from years earlier, when she had asked her mother about Grandfather.

"He does not come to us," her mother had said. "Your grandfather did not want he who was your father to marry outside of his people."

Desert Flower stopped near the chief's lodge, stood close to the slanted wall of branches, and listened.

"Your granddaughter has strong medicine," she heard White Cloud say. "Many of our children suffered from the white man's 'rotten stomach,' and Desert Flower alone survived. I wish to keep her. She might someday reveal the secret of her healing. Still, our village has so little food that I fear without a relative to provide for her, she might starve."

"A wise man does not mistake what is, for what he wishes to be," Gray Fox complimented. "I will take the child. She will never know hunger while there is breath in my body."

"It is good," White Cloud said. "Too many of our children cry from empty bellies."

Desert Flower froze. *I will never see my friends again. I should run and hide in the bushes along the creek! But what if the warriors find me? They will be angry and hurt me. Better to stay here...I am not strong enough to fight them...but I could be someday.*

After a long pause, Gray Fox said, "I am grieved to hear this. Yet I do not understand why your people have no food in the Season of Growing."

"For many seasons the fever has ravaged our village," White Cloud explained in an anguished tone. "Most of our men are dead or near dying. The few who can hunt bring back little game. That leaves us only what plant food the women and children can gather or grow. So, I allow the white-eyes passage through our land in exchange for food and blankets. Still, we never have enough for everyone—"

"You would fall to the enemy without so much as a fight?" Gray Fox interrupted, disgust in his voice.

"If I had not bargained with them, many of my people would have died."

"The white-eyes are liars! They do not pass through our land; they have come to stay. Their sod huts grow like poison mushrooms in the forest. Every Apache knows they do not give. They only take!"

The white-eyes must be very dangerous, Desert Flower thought. *Mother had always kept me away from them.*

White Cloud gently replied, "I have witnessed their foul lies, too. This time it will be different, though, for the Great White Father in Washington has sworn on his Black Book."

"The White Father's promises nourish the ears, not the stomach. The Chiricahua hunger for meat, not words. Are you White Mountain Apaches so different?"

"No—we are all brothers in hunger. But 'Three Star' has marked his words on this paper."

Desert Flower heard a rustling sound.

Gray Fox snorted. "See if that paper keeps the children from starving when the Moon of Hunger visits your village. Speaking of white-eyes' gifts, who do you think gave your people the fever?" Met with silence, Gray Fox's voice rose in anger. "You should have sent a messenger to me before you conceded to the enemy!"

"It was not an easy decis—"

"We needed to unite from the beginning and fight them off together. Now it may be too late."

"Their weapons and numbers were far greater than ours," White Cloud calmly said.

"Other chiefs would also have fought at our side. Now, because you did not fight, we might all fall and be forgotten."

Whipping open the hide, Gray Fox emerged from the lodge. His eyes locked on Desert Flower, and he seemed to recognize her. She gasped—horrified. *Run!* a voice within her urged, but she could not. Cowering in fear, she backed away, but he snatched her up in his powerful hands.

"I want to stay here!" she cried repeatedly as he carried her away, pinching her arms painfully and slinging her onto the big, black stallion.

The warriors steered their horses around, preparing to ride off. Desert Flower, wobbling on the stallion's moving back, found herself surrounded. Gray Fox pulled his lance from the ground and slid easily onto his mount, and the horses began walking.

"Stop, stop! I do not want to go!" she shrieked. Gray Fox and his warriors whistled sharply, and the horses sprinted forward.

Desert Flower lunged with her right hand and grabbed the stallion's mane, while her rear vaulted back onto his hindquarters. As she pulled herself forward, she bounced again and nearly slipped off the left side. Pummeled by the horse's jolting back, she clamped onto more of the mane with her left hand. Straining both arms, she brought her legs up under her. She wriggled ahead until her legs straddled the lowest part of the horse's back and regained her balance.

Desert Flower gradually adjusted to the up-and-down flow of the stallion's gait. Her fists and arms aching, she looked for a place to hold higher on the mane, saw the earth speeding beneath her, grew dizzy, and squeezed her eyes shut. She drew deep, ragged breaths until the lightheadedness passed. Opening her eyes, she looked around. Behind her, to her dismay, the smoke from the village fires had receded nearly out of sight. Horror stories flashed through her mind of enemy tribes taking children as slaves. She remembered her mother warning her not to play beyond the village: *If you are captured, you will never return.*

Desert Flower was so frightened, she did not care when warm fluid gushed from her bladder, soaking her dress and the stallion's back. She begged the warriors to take her home, but they kept the horses at a full gallop. Before long, she grew hoarse and could no longer hear her own pleading. Giving herself over to total desperation, she wrapped her spindly arms around the stallion's neck and hung on for dear life.

On and on they rode. The sun and wind burned her face and arms, and the constant grinding of her legs against the horse's back had rubbed her skin raw. Her stomach roiled in pain, and her muscles cramped from constantly trying to stay balanced on the horse's bouncing back. Father Sun arced above them and began his descent. *How far will they take me? Will this nightmare ever end?*

The Chiricahua warriors did not fear the faint-hearted White Mountain people, but Gray Fox, now aware of their alliance with the Bluecoats, considered the territory dangerous. Part of him actually hoped to come upon a small platoon of soldiers so he could acquire one of their new repeating rifles. But he would not risk a fight, especially while his only grandchild rode with him.

His mood brightened once they entered Chiricahua territory. The warriors slowed their horses and began to tease one another. Gray Fox smiled over his shoulder. "These hills are beautiful, do you not agree, Desert Flower?"

She scowled at him in silence, thinking how much she disliked her name, especially in the company of these warriors. *Desert flowers are soft. I do not want to be soft and helpless.* She stared at the untamed land, noticing the irregular, green-forested hills ahead.

"Yes," she responded hoarsely. She recalled how he had abused her throughout the day. Leaning forward, she hugged the stallion's neck and whispered in his ear, "I hate this country and my grandfather, too. I hate him, I hate him, I hate him!"

Gray Fox hurried them along as the sun sank toward the underworld. He wanted to reach Prairie Dog Creek before dark, an excellent place to camp.

When they arrived, the men dismounted and walked along the creek, stretching their legs and bending their backs. Desert Flower stayed on her horse.

"Come on down," Gray Fox said in a pleasant voice. When she ignored him, he walked closer and softly told her again. She did not know how to dismount, so she remained sitting, her dark, explosive eyes fixed intently upon the distant hills.

Not accustomed to such arrogance, Gray Fox grabbed her by the arm and tugged. When the swift jerk failed to unseat her, she kicked at him. His temper flared, and he reached for her again. Grasping her waist, he wrenched her to the ground. Instantly his face contorted, and he hissed when he recognized the foul smell emanating from her clothing. He picked her up—paying no attention to her caterwauling —and dumped her into the shallow creek.

Desert Flower wailed loudly enough to wake the ancients. The fierce-looking warriors laughed and covered their ears with their hands, attempting to protect themselves from her ear-bursting screams. When she finally quieted, a young brave rose and began clapping his hands in appreciation of the show.

"Her voice is like thunder," the brave commented.

"On that, Soaring Hawk, we agree." Gray Fox smiled without humor.

Chilled to the bone, Desert Flower waded out of the water and sat alone on the sandy riverbank. *I hate Chiricahuas*, she thought, sulking. She remembered the urge to run that morning. *I will show them. I will wait until they are all sleeping, then take the black horse and go home.*

Rubbing her sore buttocks, she remembered Chief White Cloud's concern for her. *If I go home, I may starve.* She would search out another tribe. Yes, she would find a small band that loved children. A respected warrior wearing at least ten eagle feathers in his hair would live among them. He and his wife would adopt her. Desert Flower would astound the men and boys with her beauty, and the women with her strength and wisdom. These people would bring her gifts of food and clothing decorated with exquisite designs. A tall, handsome brave would plead with her to marry him, assuring her that as the wife of the chief's son, she would have wealth and respect.

Tangled in her make-believe, she failed to notice Gray Fox's approach until he draped a deerskin robe around her shoulders. She snatched it off, flinging it at his feet.

"What are you doing, child?" he scolded. "It gets cold in these mountains at night, and you will freeze in those wet clothes."

Desert Flower shot him a quizzical glance. "*You* just threw me in the creek! Why do you care about me now?"

Gray Fox ignored the outburst and handed her a rawhide pouch about the size of her hand. "Come, small one," he said. "Sit by the fire and have some of our pemmican."

Spurred by hunger, Desert Flower glared at him as she grabbed the pouch. She followed Gray Fox to the fire, sat, and devoured the dried meat and berries.

She listened to the warriors vying for prestige, telling tales of past battles and raids when they counted coup to show their courage.

She knew warriors counted coup in several ways. One might touch an enemy in battle and escape unharmed or steal his weapons or horses. But she had never heard stories of such bravery and daring as these from the men of her own village.

When her eyes grew heavy, she maneuvered herself closer to the fire. *I can always run away tomorrow.*

Soon the night sounds faded, leaving Desert Flower in a world of soft silence. Sometime during the night, a mist fell, soaking her robe and chilling her bones. She pulled the robe tighter, wishing she were back in her village with her mother to keep her warm. *Your mother is with the star people,* her spirit whispered, *and you must learn to take care of yourself.* The dark silhouettes of the sleeping warriors across the sodden camp contrasted starkly with the memory of her mother. Drawing a ragged breath, she summoned the loving memory by looking at the dim outline of her only piece of jewelry, a bracelet of various shades of turquoise.

Mother was very ill. She spent many days carefully chipping holes through each berry-sized stone. She strung the stones together and tied it around my wrist.

"Mother, this is too loose for me."

She smiled. "You will grow into it."

She died later that day.

Desert Flower wept as she ran her fingers along the beads, remembering her mother. At last, sleep came to her.

Father Sun had just peeped over the edge of the earth when Gray Fox shook her awake. Groaning, she tried to stand. She trembled as pain seeped down her spine and spilled into her legs.

Gray Fox frowned and tried to help her to her feet. "Are you sick?" Genuine concern etched his face.

"I was sick, Grandfather, as Chief White Cloud told you. And now my back and legs are cramped from riding all day." She saw the nearby braves eating pemmican and listening.

Gray Fox smiled. "I thought you were eavesdropping on us. But why would—?"

"It was my first time riding a horse," she cut in, speaking softly for fear the braves might hear and start laughing again. "My village had few horses."

"We Chiricahua teach our children to ride horseback by their fourth winter. Also, Chief White Cloud spoke as if you had completely recovered. We needed to leave his land quickly, or Blue-coats might have seen us. Had I known the extent of your weakness, I would not have ridden so far without stopping to rest."

"Weakness?" Desert Flower snapped. "I will ride harder today!" She hobbled toward the black stallion.

The braves stopped eating and sat with puzzled looks. Grinning slightly, Gray Fox took his things and Desert Flower's wet robe, then told the others, "Let us go. It seems she is ready to ride."

Desert Flower stood on her tiptoes, clutching fistfuls of the horse's mane, ready to try to pull herself up, when Grandfather appeared next to her.

"There is an easier way," he said, lightly placing his hand on her shoulder and drawing her away from the stallion. He stepped to a patch of tall grass, cut off a fistful with his knife, and returned. Speaking to the horse gently, he fed him the grass, lowered his hand, and brought the horse's head nearly to the ground.

He looked at Desert Flower. "Come, press your legs against his neck and bend over it." She did so, and he held her elbow to steady her. As the stallion's head began to rise, Gray Fox said tenderly, "Swing your leg around his neck and slide down." When she reached the animal's back, she began to slip off to the other side. Gray Fox tugged her toward him, centering her on the horse. He looked up to her. "When you want to dismount, just grab his mane and lift your leg over his hindquarters. As soon as your feet swing down, let go of the mane and drop to the ground."

Desert Flower tried not to grimace as her sore legs settled on the stallion's back. Her people's stories of children becoming slaves ran through her mind. Although she disliked the Chiricahuas, she could not bear the thought of becoming a slave. She must try to get along with these callous warriors.

Gray Fox handed her another pouch of pemmican.

Desert Flower grinned. "Thank you, Grandfather." She took a bite and put the rest in her pocket.

Gray Fox patted her knee. "If you need anything, speak to me."

Desert Flower's eyes smiled as she nodded.

While they rode, the warm sun and light breeze dried Desert Flower's hair and dress quickly. Feeling much better, she let her thoughts drift to her plan to run away. *I do not want to go to a new tribe. They will not accept me. But I never had enough food in our village, and Grandfather is providing for me.* She looked ahead and sighed. *It is best to obey Grandfather and try to join his people.*

The sun had climbed high when Desert Flower saw the village from afar. Dome-shaped, thickly thatched wikiups stood everywhere, woven neatly amid a dense stand of cottonwood trees. As the riders drew nearer, a group of excited children surrounded by a pack of barking dogs ran out to greet them. Not far behind came the adults. Everyone seemed eager to meet the *nantan*'s granddaughter.

The black stallion stopped at the edge of the village. Following Grandfather's instructions, Desert Flower grabbed the horse's mane and tried to dismount. She swayed down much faster than expected, and her momentum began to swing her up again. The stallion raised his head and whinnied.

"Sorry, my friend," she whispered, and let go of the mane. She dropped to the ground and stumbled backward a few steps. Her tender muscles bawled in pain as she brought herself back to balance and turned toward the villagers.

The people laughed at her clumsy dismount but soon quieted. Many women stared at her, and children gaped as though she were a ghost. She met the gaze of a solemn-faced boy of about eleven winters. He was tall for his age, and his unusual dark gray eyes seemed to smile at her. Thankful for the kind look, she returned the smile. Desert Flower rubbed the big stallion's neck. Only the horse, Grandfather, and the boy seemed not intimidated by her status as the chief's reclaimed granddaughter.

Frightened by the strange village, she could neither control her quaking limbs nor stop worrying thoughts from pecking at her mind. *What if they do not accept me?* She stared in the direction of the far-off White Mountains and wished she still lived amid those ashen giants.

Desert Flower's illness among the White Mountain tribe had stolen her strength, and every muscle in her body ached. But as she began her life in her new tribe, she instinctively disguised her pain behind expressionless eyes. Yet while in solitude, her silent tears often dampened her blanket. Some nights, her legs ached so fiercely she refused to sleep, afraid of crying out like an undisciplined, troublesome baby. Somehow, Grandfather always knew. When she could endure no more, he would massage her feet and legs with an evil-smelling ointment until the pain subsided.

Aware of her duties, Desert Flower washed Grandfather's clothing, cleaned his lodge, and cooked for him. Grandfather taught her how to care for his horses, and that too became her responsibility. She particularly enjoyed her time with the black stallion. While looking after him, she often spoke to him, and he seemed to understand.

She missed her White Mountain Apache people. Feeling like an outsider among the Chiricahuas, she made no effort to truly join the tribe but simply went about her chores. Recalling her friends, she wished she were back in her former village. Yet, if she had stayed, she might have already died of starvation. She winced at the thought.

As part of Desert Flower's assimilation into the Chiricahua people, Gray Fox planned a naming ceremony for her. One evening, under a rising full moon, the nearly one hundred villagers gathered for a celebration dance. Afterward, Gray Fox told the story of her first time riding a horse, and how she yelled like thunder. Everyone laughed along with Desert Flower.

Smiling, Gray Fox proclaimed her new name: "Talks Like Thunder."

The crowd gave a resounding cheer, and Gray Fox ended the ceremony. *Talks Like Thunder,* she repeated within. *No longer will others speak of me as a frail flower...*

The tribe formed a line, and one by one, the adults and children welcomed Talks Like Thunder into the village. For the first time, she felt part of her new people. *I cannot go back to my friends in the White Mountains. I must make my new home here and new friends. I will try.* A warmth from within reassured her.

That night, in her wickiup during the first storm of the summer season, Thunder lay awake as her mighty namesake shook the earth. An inexplicable power pulsed inside her, and she realized her grandfather really did care about her. He had even given her the name of the great divine voice, Thunder. She lifted her thoughts to the mountain spirits and prayed her soul would find contentment among her new people.

Thunder had great difficulty during her first days in the youngsters' hunting and weapons training. One morning as she struggled to string her bow, a girl of about nine winters walked to her.

"Let me help you, Thunder," she said.

"Thank you." Thunder handed her the bow.

The girl smiled. "My name is Young Falcon." She placed one end of the bow against the ground, then bent down and picked up the string. "We must keep our weapons in ideal condition to fight the white-eyes, so make sure to string your bow tight. The tension makes arrows fast and accurate."

"Why do we call the invaders white-eyes?"

"Because even their eyes are pale." Young Falcon pointed at one of her own eyes, at the lighter part outside the iris. "This part is pure white, much lighter than ours. It is strange." She pulled the bow down and deftly tied the string to the top.

Wondering about the boy with gray eyes who smiled at her when she first arrived at the village Thunder asked about him.

"He must be Sparrow," Young Falcon responded. "His father is Grinning Bear, the leader of the Warrior Society. Grinning Bear sees to the warrior training of all boys once they have twelve winters. He teaches them ways to hide their tracks, mimic birdcalls to communicate, and many other warrior skills. She who was Sparrow's mother died years ago." Without a break, Young Falcon returned to her lesson. "We should always attack before nightfall because of dew. It makes our bowstrings soften, and the arrows will not fly straight."

"You seem to know almost everything," Thunder said, impressed.

Young Falcon smiled and returned the bow to Thunder. "Before an attack, we always perform a ritual of asking the spirits to bless our bows and ourselves."

Thunder was fascinated by the beads adorning the leather strings tied to the ends of Young Falcon's braids. "I have never seen such ivory beads. Where did you get them?"

"My family's beads are very old. After she who was my grandmother died two winters ago, my mother gave them to me. I, too, will wear them until I die."

Thunder admired Young Falcon's sentiment toward her grandmother and resolved to show her own mother the same regard. Many times, her mother had gone without food so Thunder could have enough. Thunder rubbed the keepsake on her wrist. *I will always wear my bracelet in honor of my mother.*

During the following moons, Grandfather encouraged Thunder to develop her hunting skills, so she spent most of her time practicing with her knife and bow. Young Falcon helped her, and the two became close. The other girls were all a few years older and none too friendly. They yelled encouragement to each other but constantly ridiculed the much smaller Thunder for her scrawniness. Young Falcon defended her but could do little against so many. Thunder wanted to explain that sickness had caused her gaunt body, but Grandfather had forbidden her to mention it. "Never speak of the white man's rotten stomach," he had cautioned, "or you could draw the evil fever to our village." So, she suffered their taunts in silence.

One day, while Thunder shot arrows at targets, the older girls swooped in and began to tease her. "Pretending to be a warrior shooting those arrows?" a girl hissed.

Thunder hated nothing more than feeling helpless. "I am practicing for hunting!" she answered, her voice shaking from embarrassment.

"Because you are so spindly you will never find a man to hunt for you?" another girl jeered.

"I do not need a man to best all of you!" Thunder screamed, swinging her loaded bow toward the girls.

"Stop!" came a male voice from behind Thunder. She lowered her bow and froze. Sparrow ran up behind her with two companions. He chased the girls off. "If I catch any of you bothering Thunder again, there will be trouble. Leave her alone!"

When they were out of sight, Thunder thanked Sparrow.

"I had to stop them," he said. "When one of us is tormented, it brings discord to us all."

Sparrow's two friends passed by with a nod. "Crossing Wolf, Two Feathers, and I are going hunting." He looked at Thunder's target. "One landed dead center. Keep it up. It will not be long before those girls fear you." He winked at her. "If they bother you again, tell me."

"I will."

From that day on, Sparrow treated Thunder with particular courtesy. She guessed he, having lost his mother, understood the hardships of losing parents. He had a quick and easy smile, and from time to time, he would say silly things to make her laugh. He had four more winters than she did, and she looked up to him. They spoke to each other often and soon became good friends.

As Thunder learned the skills of weapons and hunting, Grandfather taught her about other aspects of life. Each morning, they would chant their prayers in the forest as Father Sun came to light the eastern sky.

"The sun," Grandfather explained, "is the life-giver, the father of all. His passage through the sky within the four sacred directions governs our lives. His crossing from east to west divides night from day and his journey from south to north and back again divides the seasons. To show our gratitude to the powers that provide us with life, we must give them prayers and offerings."

Grandfather taught her which plants were edible and which had curative properties. He told her the name of every creature in the wild and instructed her on the animals' significance in the universe. Fascinated by this new teaching, Thunder absorbed it quickly. Although she disliked killing, and avoided hunting whenever possible, she accepted it as necessary to meet the basic needs of survival.

Grandfather also regularly took Thunder out at night, and she soon learned the position of the North Star and the phases of the moon. He told her if she could see those, they would guide her in any direction at night. As the moons passed, she and Grandfather began observing the other stars. With Grandfather's help, she learned the stars slowly crept past the sun in the sky, night after night. Thus, different stars appeared at night during each season. "When you cannot see the moon, but you see stars and know when in the year they shine," Grandfather said, "you will know the time of night."

TWO

New Mexico Territory, April 1876

The winters passed as rapidly as an arrow flies. Grandfather's promise to never let Thunder go hungry allowed her to outgrow her thinness and bloom into her full being. Through years of honing her knife and bow accuracy, her use of weapons had surpassed that of her peers. The vigorous Apache discipline rewarded Thunder with strength and dexterity.

One day early in her twelfth spring, Thunder returned home to find Grinning Bear sitting with her grandfather. After they exchanged greetings, Grandfather smiled and invited Thunder to join them.

Warriors seldom speak to girls formally, Thunder thought as she took her seat. *Why would Grinning Bear want to speak to me?*

"You have great skill with weapons," Grinning Bear said, "and I think you belong in the Warrior Society. I invite you to begin training with the young men tomorrow morning."

Thunder was dumbfounded by the invitation. Such a possibility had never before crossed her mind. "But women do not become warriors."

"We have no women warriors now," Grandfather broke in, "but we have in the past." He looked at Grinning Bear, then back to Thunder. "Daughter," he said, warming her heart with his name of endearment for her, "it is a great honor for a girl to be chosen as a warrior. Not many can boast of such an achievement. The white-eyes are everywhere now, and your duty is to protect your people. We have only the young warriors to ensure Apache blood will continue to flow in generations to come."

Thunder wondered what Sparrow would think. *Would he be proud, or would he consider me strange?* She did not want to spoil her chances of a deeper relationship with him. "But Grandfather," she protested, "young braves do not look to women warriors when choosing a wife."

"Do not concern yourself about a husband. Many moons must pass before I will allow one to claim you."

Although he spoke softly, Thunder recognized the finality in his tone. Grandfather had never punished her or even raised his voice to her, but she knew it was useless to try to change his mind.

She remembered wanting to become like the Chiricahua warriors the day Grandfather took her from the White Mountains. *Maybe I can be a warrior! And I will have the chance to see Sparrow more often.* Unbidden, a faint smile crept to her face.

Grinning Bear stood, looked at Thunder, and said, "I will see you at sunrise."

Thunder had not realized how demanding she would find warrior training. Besides improving her bowmanship, she had to join the young men in athletic competitions, long runs, and mock combat. She also needed to master the making and use of rock slings, spears, and lances. So, like the others, Thunder spent part of her days carefully chipping flint for weapon tips. Grinning Bear took great patience in teaching them to replicate his unique designs.

Thunder strove to learn fighting skills quickly but struggled to keep up with the others. Still, everyone knew no other girl had attempted the rigorous warrior discipline in many years. One and all treated her with respect, including her first-year companions, Silver Leaf and Firemaker.

Blood Moon, a warrior known for his hot temper, assisted Grinning Bear, working mostly with the first-year apprentice warriors—the novices. He told Thunder, Silver Leaf, and Firemaker they must learn to treat wounds: their own and those of others. Thus, when someone in the village had a bad injury, they would observe the craft of the village healer, Sunflower.

On their first visit, the novices found the old woman treating a young girl with swelling in the arch of her foot. She had stepped on a sharp stick days before. Sunflower used a thin flint to dig deeply into the wound and pull out two large slivers. She told the novices what herbs she used as she prepared and applied them.

Similar healings occurred with each visit. Sunflower spoke with the wisdom of her age and experience, always teaching as she worked. The novices learned how to clean wounds, stop bleeding, and which herbs were best for ailments and injuries.

With the help of Grandfather and the Warriors' Society, Thunder mastered many secrets of the forest and desert. She could weave a basket, build a rabbit snare, and make a bow and arrow in less than a day. Although skilled in the ways of the wilderness, she most valued the knowledge she obtained from observing the animals themselves. She would lie for the entire morning, scarcely batting an eye or twitching a muscle, until every animal in the forest accepted her presence. Mastering patience, Grandfather said, would serve her well in life, especially as a warrior.

Grandfather taught Thunder the higher concepts of the Apache. He explained how Ussen, the supreme deity, had created the universe and existed as part of everything in it. Ussen created White Painted Woman and sent her down to the world to live. Lightning fathered White Painted Woman's son, Child of the Water. In time, Child of the Water grew and eventually slew the great monsters of the world's early days. During that time, White Painted Woman gave rise to the Apache people.

Grandfather taught Thunder all living entities have souls. Their knowledge was different from that of people—they knew less in some ways, more in others. He taught her the difference between the soul and the body and stressed the importance of understanding her own nature.

As the moons passed and the season turned to summer, Blood Moon introduced the novices to the most accurate and deadly weapons— pistols and rifles. All other weapons would be unnecessary if one could kill the enemy with guns from a distance. Thunder began training with enthusiasm, wanting to quickly master this new skill.

One day, Sparrow helped her with target practice after training. On their way home, he asked her what she had learned lately. She talked about healing and herbs, and that Grandfather had told her patience made her a better warrior.

"If you are mastering patience and becoming a warrior," Sparrow said with a seriousness he seldom expressed, "you should also begin to master pain. Face the pain without fearing it. If an enemy wounds you in battle, you must keep on fighting until you are safe."

Intrigued, Thunder asked, "How can I do that?"

"There is a warrior part of your spirit that you need to call on in battle. We need to let it take over our minds. It helps us endure the wounds we cannot treat until the enemy is gone."

"Once the warrior spirit manifests, it never leaves?"

"It comes and goes, but it should grow within you as you train. I remember your tale of the long ride from your White Mountain Apache home to our village. Now you can run that far easily in a day, finding shortcuts riders cannot pass. You never thought you could, but now you can. So, it will be with the greater achievements."

As the seasons changed, so did Talks Like Thunder. She became robust; her fragile arms and legs thickened and hardened with muscle. Her bronze skin glittered like white-eyes' gold, a stone the Apache called "Ussen's tears."

Thunder enjoyed the privilege of her novice status, pleased she did not have to braid her hair as the other girls did but could let it flow loosely to her hips. She also relished knowing she could run as fast and shoot as accurately as any of her peers. She began to feel the power Sparrow spoke about. She felt less pain when testing her body's limits, and satisfaction grew within as the fear of pain decreased over time.

THREE

New Mexico Territory, October 1876

Early one evening, Soaring Hawk and Crossing Wolf returned from patrolling the Chiricahua territory with bad news. A group of settlers, encroaching on Chiricahua land, had provoked a fight with the two warriors. As the warriors drove off the white thieves, they took five Apache horses and headed north toward a settlers' village

The next morning, Thunder took an armful of clothes to the stream. She and Young Falcon washed clothing together every few days. Since Soaring Hawk was courting Young Falcon, Thunder hoped to learn more about the horse theft from her.

Squatting on a fallen tree barely above water, Thunder dunked the buckskin clothes and slapped them against the barkless trunk, brooding. *Someone should at least try to get our horses back.*

Young Falcon arrived, carrying clothes and glowing with delight.

"What makes you so happy?" Thunder asked. "Soaring Hawk?"

Young Falcon nodded and shared that for almost a moon, they had been slipping out of the village almost every night, walking in the forest under the moonlight. She hoped Soaring Hawk would want to marry her and ask his parents to help provide a dowry.

Thunder plunged the buckskin into the water and looked at her friend. "You both come from good families. It may take a few moons for Soaring Hawk's parents to obtain your dowry of horses, but that time will pass soon enough."

"That is just what I needed to hear. Thunder, you are such a good friend."

Young Falcon wrung out her dress. "If I get married, we will have a new lodge near Soaring Hawk's family. You and I will be as close as ever."

Thunder smiled. "I am so glad everything is going well for you."

"I am a little worried about Soaring Hawk, though. He is cleaning his rifle to lead a raid to recover the horses tomorrow, and it sounds dangerous—"

"A raid!" Thunder dropped the buckskin and sprang up, almost slipping off the wet log. "Why did you not tell me earlier?"

"I never thought you would be considered. You are still in early training."

"I can help get the horses back. Who is going with him?"

"Crossing Wolf, Horse Walker, and two others."

"I will be back soon."

Before Young Falcon could respond, Thunder hopped off the log and ran to the village.

Soaring Hawk put the rifle down when Thunder approached. After they greeted each other, Thunder sat facing him. Soaring Hawk smiled. "Your progress since we brought you from the White Mountain village has impressed me."

The compliment surprised Thunder. "Thank you. My mind is set on becoming a warrior, and I want to learn as fast as I can." Thunder took a deep breath and continued. "I would like to join in the raid."

Soaring Hawk hesitated before answering. "We need one more volunteer, and no one else has come forward. So, I will consider this a special case. Since Sparrow, the most experienced apprentice warrior, will also go, I will permit you, despite your youth. But you must do exactly what Sparrow tells you."

"I will and thank you." Thunder smiled within at the thought of Sparrow riding with her. "I will do my best to help the warriors."

"You and Sparrow will not take part in the raid and will not carry guns. You will care for the horses, fetch water, and stand guard while I and the other warriors sleep. You must stay hidden while we warriors slip into the whites' town at dawn. We will find our stolen horses without rousing the settlers and ride them to you. Together, we will ride back to our village. If the raid does not go well, you and Sparrow must return here with the horses."

Thunder agreed to the task and left, excited and determined to prove herself. A mysterious, warm tingle flowed through her body as she walked back to Young Falcon. *It feels good to have Sparrow at my side and guide me through my first encounter with the enemy.* She remembered Sparrow in training—never rash, always clear-headed, strategic, calculating, no wasted blows or shots. Not only did she trust him as a friend, but also as a reliable fighter.

That night, Thunder told Grandfather that Soaring Hawk had allowed her to go on the raid. Concern flashed across his face; he shook his head and glared at her. "It is too soon for you to go into enemy territory."

Thunder cringed at his reaction. "But Grandfather," she said meekly, "I have already promised Soaring Hawk I would participate. I cannot take back my promise now."

Gray Fox's eyes stayed locked on hers. "You do not know the danger."

"Only Sparrow and I volunteered."

Grandfather blinked. "Sparrow defending you is some comfort. Still, I would rather take the loss of five horses than put your life at risk."

Thunder reached out and took his hand. "Grandfather, I am ready to test my skills."

He put his other hand over hers. "Daughter, you are barely trained, but I cannot reason with you. Take the black stallion. The tribe's most disciplined and prized horse may protect you."

Thunder nodded in agreement, but Grandfather's response made her anxious for what lay ahead.

The next day, after a long journey, the seven Apaches stopped slightly below the crest of a lone hillock north of the white men's town. Sparrow and Thunder crawled to the top and looked to the valley. There, for the first time, she saw the square buildings of the whites.

"Why do the whites make their lodges bigger than any family would ever need?" Sparrow remarked.

Thunder shrugged; she wondered the same thing herself. "Are the buildings made of dirt?"

"Yes, sunbaked dirt—it is called adobe."

They returned to the warriors and helped pitch camp on the hidden side of the crest. Finally, all but the lookouts lay down to sleep for the night.

At first light the five warriors, each carrying a rifle, left the camp on foot, blending silently into nature. Thunder and Sparrow ascended the knoll, bows in hand. They hid behind a group of boulders and looked down the slope.

Gunshots erupted, and a cloud of dust rose from below. A warrior ran out the opposite side of the town, then suddenly fell dead. Thunder cringed. *The raid has gone wrong! Soaring Hawk told us to stay hidden, but the warriors may all die!*

Thunder took a step downhill and glanced at Sparrow. "They need help."

A flash of anger shot from his eyes. "Stay right here!" he commanded.

Thunder hesitated before stepping back, hating to wait uselessly when her brothers needed aid.

Four Apaches sprinted from the town, running in different directions.

"Sparrow, we must help them now!"

"Do not move and keep quiet. We have our duty."

She clenched her jaw and obeyed, remembering her promise to Soaring Hawk.

Six white men rode after the Apaches, fanning out in pairs. *Sparrow may be right. Some could come here and find our horses.* Thunder reached into her quiver and pulled out an arrow, while Sparrow did the same.

An Apache running northwest in the open turned and shot as two riders closed in. One white man fell before the other fired, bringing the warrior to the ground.

Thunder gasped. *Two down.*

Another pair of riders sped southwest after Crossing Wolf and Soaring Hawk, who ran with a comfortable lead. The warriors jumped into a deep gully, where the whites' horses could not follow. *Good, they will outwit the whites on foot.*

The first shooter reached his two companions, and all three dismounted and jumped into the gully to chase the Apaches.

While Horse Walker ran northeast, a pair of riders stayed on him and fired. His left arm went limp as he ran into a dense thicket. The riders followed, and a rapid exchange of gunfire broke out. *Horse Walker may die like the others. Only four able-bodied left.*

Two more whites rode out from the village, directly toward Thunder and Sparrow's hiding place. *With my arrows against their guns, I will likely die!* Thunder's body began to tremble. *Stop it! I have no chance without a steady aim. Calm yourself! Warrior spirit, help me!* She took a long breath and watched the two split to pass the boulders. Sparrow drew his bow and sent a deadly arrow into the first rider's chest.

Thunder took sight on the man passing to her side. She drew deep into her calm warrior spirit, steadily pulling her bow to its fullest. *Kill him before he has a chance to shoot!* He veered toward her, ruining her bead, his rifle pointing directly at her. She re-aimed at her moving target, careful not to rush and waste her only likely shot. *I have him!* Just as she released her arrow, he fired a round, piercing her left calf. Her knee buckled, and she toppled to the ground, riled in pain.

Recalling her training, she pushed every other thought from her mind and focused on survival. Blood flowed down both sides of her calf. She pressed on the wounds and looked up to see the attacker. He lay motionless on the ground, her arrow lodged in the center of his chest.

Sparrow rushed to her side, dropping to his knees. "How bad is it?" he said, gasping.

"The bullet just hit muscle." Thunder tried to keep the panic from her voice. She could tolerate the pain, but the settlers would kill her before she could crawl over the hill to the black stallion.

"Stay still!" he ordered. "I will bind your wound."

"Bind it later. More of them will find us soon."

Sparrow looked around. "They are at a safe distance. Besides, we have more arrows." He grasped the corner of his breechcloth, ripped off a strip, and wrapped her leg snugly enough to staunch the bleeding, yet not so tightly as to cause more pain. His touch calmed Thunder beyond the comfort of binding her wound. Sparrow finished with the bandage and looked across the landscape. "The whites are all together and riding toward us," he whispered calmly. "We must leave now. I will free the horses."

He rose and sprinted over the knoll, then reappeared, riding the black stallion. When he reached Thunder, she said, "Our people need more guns. Let us take the dead settlers' rifles."

He dismounted. "The riders are too close." Grasping her firmly by the waist, Sparrow lifted her over his head onto the horse's back. He jumped on behind her, and they rode off. When they crested the hill, he whistled and the horses followed.

The settlers reached the top of the knoll and shot several rounds, then continued to chase them. The black stallion carried them at full speed for many bowshots. Thunder looked back repeatedly, watching the whites slowly disappearing from sight, until only the warriors' horses followed them. Her pulse slowed, and she released a pent-up breath. "I do not see anyone behind us."

Pulling back on the reins, Sparrow brought the horse to a gentle canter. "Can you bear the pain?"

Her leg bounced against the horse, throbbing. The bandage, now tight around the wound, oozed blood from both sides. *I should raise the leg to start its healing and ease the pain, but best to wait until we are safely back in the village.* "Yes, I can bear it."

Through the corner of her eye, she saw him grin.

"If it gets worse, we can stop to rest. Otherwise, we will be home by nightfall."

"I am glad you got me out of there."

"I would never have left you behind. Besides, it is part of the warrior code."

"I know, but I am still glad."

"Sometimes caring for the wounded matters more than anything else we do. We lost two warriors, and we cannot send their souls home. But we could not have helped them. The whites would have killed us as well. When nothing else can be done, you can only wait until the battle is over. Then you can aid the wounded."

"How will I know when I should wait?"

"Sometimes it is not clear. Other times, like today, it is beyond all doubt. The best we could do was bring the wounded home. The warriors will protect one another as they return, and I will do the same for you."

The failure of the raid disappointed the Chiricahua villagers. Nonetheless, that night at the campfire, Gray Fox spoke of his gratitude to Sparrow. "It took sharp eyes, strength, and quick wit to bring my injured granddaughter back to safety. Thus, you have proven your capabilities as a warrior. Your actions resemble those of the golden eagle, and this shall be your warrior name."

Sparrow—now Golden Eagle—stood proudly silent.

Thunder sat near the two, her leg still aching, though Sunflower had treated and bandaged it earlier. She beamed, proud of her friend, happy he was receiving the recognition he deserved. She decided to make Golden Eagle a friendship medallion to thank him.

The next day, Horse Walker straggled in, arm in a sling and bandaged, head down and shoulders slumped. He walked with Soaring Hawk on his left side and Crossing Wolf locking arms on his right.

The following morning, an elderly woman died in her family's lodge after a long illness. Her loss, so soon after the warriors' deaths, caused everyone to worry they had somehow offended the nearby spirits.

Aware of the people's concern, Gray Fox announced, "We will move to a more protected area, higher into the mountains. Leave the dead and the wikiup untouched."

Once the people had packed and were ready to go. Grandfather carefully lifted Thunder onto the black stallion's back.

As Thunder and the tribe started up the mountain, she felt at ease. The smooth stride of the stallion caused her leg no pain, and it seemed she and the black stallion were made for each other. She wanted to make him her own. *But he is not. Maybe if I ask Grandfather? It would be improper; the black stallion is too valuable.* Thunder enjoyed the long ride, sharing her passing thoughts with the stallion.

After arriving, the Apaches erected a new village and posted guards day and night. As before, the Chiricahua set up the village near a stream, with training grounds for warriors and good grazing land. Soon, everyone had settled into the new encampment.

Settlers to the east lay close to the Apaches' village, limiting their hunting grounds. With the people low on food, Gray Fox took ten women, and many young warriors, including Golden Eagle, on a hunt in the Sangre de Cristo Mountains. The month of Golden Eagle's absence left Thunder distraught, but the endeavor paid off. The party returned, under the cover of darkness, with good meat and fine hides. With soldiers and settlers littering the countryside, they had not dared travel in daylight. Worried about seeing so many whites, they wondered how long they could stay hidden.

~

Four moons later, the bullet wound in Thunder's calf had healed. Sunflower had done all she could to stretch Thunder's calf muscles and return her leg to its former pliability. However, the remnants of the injury ran deep. "The scar tissue will restrict your running ability," Sunflower finally told Thunder. "I'm sorry, but I can do nothing more."

Thunder nodded but did not speak; this would change her life forever. Running fast was at the heart of being a warrior. *Retreating, giving chase, out-enduring the enemy over days; now I can be no more than a second-rate warrior. No! Sunflower is old and wise, but she doesn't know everything. I can already walk and trot easily. I will somehow find a way to run as I could before. I can do it.*

The next day, Thunder, Firemaker, and Silver Leaf arrived at the training grounds, expecting to begin tracking lessons. However, Grinning Bear abruptly announced a new training exercise. He, Blood Moon, and some other warriors would lead the novices deep into the woods, where the warriors would hide, and the novices would have three days to find them.

Everyone started for the forest, and Thunder walked with them, confounded. *How can we track them when they have not yet taught us how?*

The novices stayed in safe calling distance of one another using what skills they knew to track the warriors down. When they heard slightly odd-sounding birdcalls, leaves shaking, or twigs snapping, they would chase the sounds and find tracks, but lose them in a few hundred paces. The way the warriors toyed with them filled Thunder with dismay. She frowned. *How can they be so good? I feel more helpless than a fawn preyed on by wolves; not even they hunt with such cunning. If my teachers were enemies, I would be dead.*

By the end of the second day, the novices had all but given up.

Shortly after nightfall, Grinning Bear and his warriors found them in the moonlight. He led them back to the village, relieving them from further embarrassment.

Blood Moon stopped everyone at the training grounds and looked at the novices. "What have you learned?"

Firemaker spoke up. "You always knew exactly where we were."

Grinning Bear stepped forward. "We wanted you to know what it is like to be our enemy. If you cannot hide your tracks and find your enemy's, you are defenseless. For the next few moons, we will teach you how to out-track, outrun, and outsmart the enemy. How to plan against the enemy many steps ahead." He paused for a moment. "Return here at dawn."

The exhausted novices started to their homes.

Thunder trudged along, thinking about the exercise. She concluded that her physical conditioning and weapon skills left her no match for warriors like these. She needed to master the training to come, and above all, to learn how to outsmart the enemy.

April 1877

Late one afternoon in Thunder's thirteenth spring, she came into womanhood.

Thunder found Sunflower conversing with Bluebird outside her home. Becoming aware of the occasion, Bluebird left to make preparations. Then, Sunflower brought Thunder into her lodge.

Once both were seated, Sunflower looked at Thunder and smiled. "Today your childhood has ended, and you will receive all the rights and privileges of a woman. Your grandfather has asked me to hold a coming-of-age celebration for you. Few events in your life signify more to us than the arrival of your first menstrual cycle. The time of bleeding endows you with a great, special power. However, that power could also contaminate a warrior's weapons, or even spoil a hunt or raid. Therefore, you must remain isolated until the bleeding subsides."

Bluebird returned, and they led Thunder to a special lodge outside the village. Sunflower and the other elder women bathed and painted Thunder's body, then sprinkled sweet grass, cedar needles, and white sage on glowing coals to purify her and all involved. They clothed her in an elaborate yellow buckskin dress, the hue of pollen. Red zigzags, representing lightning, covered the dress symbolizing the force of thunder. Every family brought her food and gifts, and she was overwhelmed by their generosity.

In the following days, the attendants escorted Thunder through a myriad of rituals. She spent long sessions of dancing and kneeling vigils. Between the formalities, she received instructions from the elders concerning her new duties as a woman. They emphasized that she must remain chaste, or a man would refuse to marry her. At other times, she danced outside with her people. All this—combined with lack of sleep—utterly exhausted her.

Finally, at sunrise after the fourth night, Thunder emerged from the lodge. Performing her concluding ritual act, a ceremonial prayer to the sun, she ran eastward, toward the giver of all life.

As Thunder returned to the village, she saw a crowd of people waiting for her. In the front of the group, she saw Golden Eagle and her smiling grandfather standing next to the black stallion. When she reached Grandfather, he handed her the horse's reins and said, "He belongs to you, young woman."

"Mine?" she croaked, shocked at such a treasured gift.

Her grandfather nodded, smiling even more widely than before.

"I will call him Stormy, because thunder and storms are always together."

Everyone laughed, including Golden Eagle. He met Thunder's eyes and his expression softened into a warm and familiar smile. Her heart beat erratically. Could this be the village of her dreams, and could this be the brave who would claim her for his wife?

FOUR

New Mexico Territory, July 1877

After more than a year as novices, Thunder, Firemaker, and Silverleaf had attained the rank of apprentice warriors. Naturally, their training had grown more difficult, as had the discipline expected of them.

Thunder tried for five moons to prove Sunflower wrong about the permanence of her injury. She ran as hard as she could, then stretched and kneaded her aching calf muscles until the spasms ceased. Finally, she could run without cramping, but she still ran more slowly than the others. With a heavy heart, Thunder realized she had nearly no chance of running as well as before.

The morning Thunder knew would come finally arrived. *We apprentices must run the whole day.* She walked to the training grounds at dawn, where Blood Moon greeted her holding a pack full of rocks. She knew what it was for and turned around. As he rested it on her back, her body sagged under the load. Grinning Bear did the same to Firemaker and Silver Leaf.

Blood Moon picked up a canteen, unfastened it, then instructed Thunder to open her lips and tilt her head back. While filling her mouth, he told everyone, "Breathe through your nose, and hold the water in your mouth until you finish. Run to the mountain's base, circle The Three Hills, and return before Father Sun comes to rest."

While the three apprentices sped away, Blood Moon mounted his horse with whip in hand. Thunder kept up with the others as they passed through one landscape after another. But ever so slowly, with each stride, the boys began to pull away. The weight of the rocks caused her calf to weaken, yet she strove on. The boys passed nearly out of sight. She heard hoofbeats of Blood Moon's horse nearing and could feel his rage. A *swoosh* came through the air, and a string of pain seared her neck and arm.

"Run!" Blood Moon bellowed.

Another lash of the whip struck her rear and thighs. She wanted to stop and face him, but she continued looking ahead, determined to keep running. *Everyone knows my leg will never be the same. He hates me.*

Whack! The whip slapped over her shoulder, across her chest, and onto her thigh. Thunder grimaced from the pain and felt an unbearable urge to curse Blood Moon for his cruelty. *That is what he wants,* she warned herself. *But I will not spit out the water to speak my mind.*

"You will never become a warrior, trotting along like that! Give up now—you are not worth our time to train you." He turned his horse and rode back toward the village.

He is right. I have failed. Moons of grueling effort gone. I am unfit to be a warrior. Shame and grief overwhelmed the stinging pain of the whipping. She had never felt so detestable. *When I return to camp, I will be taunted for failing miserably. This time, I will deserve it. Golden Eagle, too, might reject me.* The ache of her lungs longing for air reminded her she was still running. Scouring the land ahead, she saw no signs of Silver Leaf and Firemaker. *Why go on? Just quit, as Blood Moon ordered. Stop, turn around, and walk back to camp. It is over. It was not my idea to be a warrior.* Her feeling of worthlessness grew, with more self-loathing than before. *What will Golden Eagle think of me if I quit? The shame will haunt me forever. No! I will not give up! Blood Moon will have to throw me out of training, and I will fight him at every turn.* Her shadow, still casting westward, informed her she had a long, grueling day to reach camp by sundown. Calling on her warrior spirit, she blocked her body's suffering and strove on.

By mid-afternoon, the countryside sweltered in the scorching sun. Sweat soaked Thunder's clothes as she rounded the final hill. She had not seen anyone since Blood Moon rode off. *Silver Leaf and Firemaker are probably back home.* She glanced at the sun. *Unlikely I will reach my village before dark. I cannot fail. I must run faster to have a chance to stay in the warrior society.*

Despite her unrelenting will, her stride had shortened, her entire body demanded she stop. Nothing was left within to keep going. *I have never been so tired. I can drop the pack and walk back home. My people will forgive my failure, and I will be accepted as a woman.* Yet deep in her being, she knew she could not live with giving up on herself.

She also desperately needed water, and yet had a mouthful of it. The air burned through her nostrils. *A rivulet ahead! Stop, drink some water, refill my mouth, and move on. Yes! No one will know. The only way to complete the run.* Approaching the tempting water, she envisioned taking a drink. *Just a few swallows…* However, she did not slow her pace. *No! Blood Moon told me to keep this water in my mouth during the run.* She leaped across the stream and scuttled on. *I will not cheat. Warrior or not, I must dwell in my own integrity.*

Shortly after dusk, Thunder lumbered into the training grounds, her mind dizzy, her body numb. Blood Moon sat alone near a campfire. She dropped her bag of rocks alongside the other packs. She locked her eyes on his and spat out the water. *Teacher or not, he better not say one word.* As she started for home, his silence goaded her. *Ignore him.* She turned her thoughts to Grandfather. *He will know everything by now. With my failure, likely he will find me intolerable too.*

Entering the wikiup, she caught a whiff of the evil-smelling ointment of years before. Grandfather beckoned her to sit near him. She saw his eyes focus on the welts on her arms as he gave her a canteen. "Lie back on these blankets."

Thunder drank ravenously from the canteen until it emptied. "Is there more?"

"No, Daughter, you have had enough for now." Still thirsty, she stayed silent and reclined. He took some salve, but instead of treating the welts, he applied it to her scarred calf. "It was a very hot day. I am curious. Did you take a drink along the route?"

"No!"

Grandfather chuckled. "I thought so."

"Why ask me that?"

"Most would have." He smiled while kneading her calf. "Often a person's deepest wound becomes her greatest strength."

What a ridiculous thing to say. "Grandfather, we both know I failed."

"You finished the run on your own accord."

"At a slow trot, and I did not return before sundown."

"You had resolve to complete the mission, though everything was against you."

Shortly after Grandfather finished treating her, she heard a greeting from outside the wikiup—Grinning Bear's voice. *He is here to cast me out from training in front of Grandfather.*

Gray Fox invited him in, and Grinning Bear sat across from them. Looking at Thunder, he said, "Blood Moon told me…" He took a deep breath.

Thunder's body tensed at the thought of Blood Moon. *I knew it! He has convinced Grinning Bear that I no longer belong with the apprentices.*

"…that you need to learn to extend your stride, which will compensate for your wound. With less burden on your injured leg, you will run faster."

He stood. "I will see you at the training grounds at dawn."

Thunder nodded and watched him leave. *They all knew. The whole thing was a test, returning by sundown, even the whipping.* She groaned, her muscles refusing to move as she lay back. *The elders are right. No warrior would have quit the race. Despite my weakened leg, I can become a better runner.* For the first time, she felt a deep contentment with herself and her warrior spirit…very happy to be who she was.

The next morning, Grinning Bear and Blood Moon, armed the apprentices with their rock slings and led them to an open field. Blood Moon ordered them to stand twenty paces apart, like the points of a triangle. Once they had taken position, he said, "Sling rocks at each other as if your life depends on it. Do not hold back. The goal is to avoid being hit."

Thunder's entire body ached from the previous day. *The teachers chose the worst time for us to engage in a rock fight.* She loaded her sling but hesitated, not wanting to hurt the other apprentices. Suddenly, a low-flying rock from Firemaker had her jumping to avoid it. Then Silver Leaf's stone rammed into her right thigh. A dull, heavy pain grew from the impact, enveloping her leg in agony. Overtaken by rage, she flung a rock at Silver Leaf, hitting him in the chest as a missile from Firemaker just missed his head. Thunder threw a stone at Firemaker, but he sidestepped it. She remembered her instructions as volleys came from the boys. It took all her ability to avoid the flying projectiles. She flung rocks back, and the two boys fought equally against her and each other. Two more missiles hit her. After some time, the three grew nimble enough to avoid nearly all the stones.

Grinning Bear called the exercise to a close and handed each of them a rifle and a pouch of bullets for target practice.

Favoring her body's bruises, Thunder plodded to the target range. As the excitement and focus of the last exercise ebbed away, she felt the ache of the previous day's run returning with every step. *My body cannot keep up with my demands.* Her warrior spirit spoke: *Press on. Walk like a warrior.* Looking ahead, pushing through her fatigue, she took the bullets from the pouch and loaded her rifle. *Today I will hit more bullseyes than ever.*

Through the warm season, Thunder's lean body rounded into gentle curves that made men and boys stare. Her raven hair hung like silk, and as she walked, its gentle swaying was like the haunting melody of a lover's flute.

Golden Eagle often stopped to talk with Thunder and Gray Fox. She was thrilled with his regular visits to her lodge and enjoyed stealing glances at him when Grandfather was not looking.

One evening, while Thunder was cooking outside her lodge, Golden Eagle came by. She smiled as they exchanged greetings and said, "Grandfather will be back soon. I found some ripe corn in the valley, and Grandfather brought back a wild turkey. Supper is almost ready, and there is plenty. Join us."

"That is good to hear. My father and I have found nothing on the hunt, and I have not eaten all day." As Golden Eagle sat, his shoulder brushed hers.

A tingle flowed through her, and a thin sheen of perspiration covered her face. "You will draw everyone's attention, sitting so close to me. Slide over."

Grinning, he leaned away from her.

Thunder's warm feeling remained, but she demurred. "What if Grandfather sees us like this?"

Golden Eagle laughed. "You seem fretful tonight. I can tell you a story to entertain you while you cook. What do you want to hear?"

"Oh, I do not know. I cannot think of anything now."

"How about 'Coyote Almost Swindles a Mare'?"

Thunder laughed. "You have convinced me. Go ahead, then."

Golden Eagle began the story. "Coyote bet a mare's owner that she would not buck, and persuaded him to prepare the horse for Coyote to ride…"

Thunder added a couple of logs to the fire, then sat and let the food cook. She soon found herself leaning against him, listening, and savoring the joy of the moment. *I will make his medallion in the image of the morning star. The brightest star in the heavens.*

The village was in heavy shadow when Golden Eagle ended his story: "…Coyote rode the mare to his village. When he ran off to bring back his friends, the untied horse simply trotted back to her owner." Golden Eagle raised an eyebrow and said, "I wish our horses had done that."

Thunder giggled. It seemed as if she could not get enough of the wonderful feeling his presence brought her. She felt his fingertips slowly slide along her arm to her shoulder. His light, tender touch gave her goosebumps. His fingers glided back down her arm toward her wrist. Suddenly his hand dropped to the ground, and he jumped to his feet, looking embarrassed.

Grandfather! Thunder realized, aghast. *Golden Eagle is tongue-tied.* She instantly stood up. *Say something.* "Supper has been waiting for you, Grandfather, and I invited Golden Eagle to eat with us."

Surprisingly, Gray Fox seemed to have no reaction to seeing them so close together. As she served them, she worried he might voice his displeasure about their behavior. However, near the end of the meal, he only spoke with gratitude, thanking Golden Eagle again for saving his granddaughter on the failed raid. Thunder knew it meant he approved of their relationship. It warmed her heart so much, she nearly began to cry.

Later, lying awake, Thunder reminisced about the evening. Her tender, carefree interaction with Golden Eagle had awakened a response in her she had never known. *I have fantasized of a brave like Golden Eagle ever since I left the White Mountain Apaches, and now my dream has become real. I did not know being with him would bring me such delight. Everything seems more alive and precious, as if I know life as it really is for the first time.*

The next afternoon, Thunder started for Young Falcon's home. Her friend had married shortly after the tribe had moved higher into the mountains, ten moons before.

When Thunder arrived, she found the materials for the fine deer-skin shirt she was embroidering as a surprise gift for Grandfather. Thunder took up her sewing, and Young Falcon settled in as well, stitching some small pieces of hide.

Thunder pointed to the buckskin. "What can you be making that is so tiny?"

Young Falcon's eyes glowed. "I am with child."

"That is wonderful!" Thunder cried, throwing her arms around her friend.

"Both families are thrilled about it."

"Naturally. I am so happy for you." Thunder paused for a moment, looking down. "And maybe a little envious. Though I know I should not be impatient."

Young Falcon grinned. "You and Golden Eagle were as close as ever only a few days ago."

"Yes, he stops by almost every day."

"Then everything should not be far off for you."

"I hope so," Thunder said, relieved. "I do not want to ever lose the feeling I have. Sometimes I worry about how I would feel if we ever separated, or if Golden Eagle lost interest in me."

Young Falcon sighed. "Oh, Thunder. That is just part of caring deeply for another person. Do not bother with such worries. Just enjoy being in love."

Thunder attended the late summer social dances. As expected of a maiden, she invited Golden Eagle to dance with her regularly throughout the evenings. Still, they were never alone.

September 1877

It had been over a moon since Grinning Bear told Thunder she needed to increase her stride, yet she did not know exactly what he meant. One morning, as she reached the training grounds, Blood Moon met her. "I have noticed your strides are too short, and you bob up and down as you run. You must change that. Run around the training ground and concentrate on flinging your legs forward."

Thunder did so and returned winded.

"Yes," Blood Moon said, "I see some improvement. Take another lap and swing your hips with the flow of your legs. You must also move your arms further forward and back.

Thunder ran another circle lengthening the stride of her arms and legs. She knew she was faltering when she returned and was afraid Blood Moon would be angry.

"I also see you sway from side to side as you run," Blood Moon said. "You must retrain yourself. Focus at one point on the horizon. If the point moves up and down or side to side, your stride is not ideal."

"Thank you, teacher," Thunder said, overflowing with gratitude that he had not given up on her. "I can do what you expect of me."

In the following days, Thunder ran with Blood Moon's instructions in mind, but time after time, she ended displeased with herself. Slowly she realized her lower back needed to twist to allow her hips to swivel and to gain precious length to each stride. As she mastered that motion, her body flowed forward without jolting or swaying. She ran faster with less effort; the point on the horizon stayed immovable. Although pleased with her progress, Thunder had to admit she was still the slowest among her peers. *Everything changed when I was shot.* She remembered Soaring Hawk and Grandfather's hesitation at her desire to join the raid. *Yes, it had been too soon. I must draw on my courage and tactics to overcome my weakness. I need to become an unyielding warrior.*

Blood Moon told the warrior apprentices they should consider testing their endurance of pain by holding their forearms over a flaming plant stalk until it burned out. He forced no one to do this, but he and other warriors all highly recommended it.

Thunder, though determined to make herself into a steely

warrior, preferred to undertake this test alone. She walked into the forest and pulled a dead giant ragweed from the ground. After peeling off the stems and leaves, cutting it to the right length, and starting a fire, Thunder prayed for strength from the spirits. She rolled up her sleeve, held the dirt of the root-ball, and put the stalk into the flame. *Like taking a wound in battle…Empty the mind and let the warrior spirit meet the pain.* When the stalk began to blaze, Thunder prayed again and put the flame under her forearm.

A hot wave of pain flooded her entire body as the heat seared her skin. She smelled burning flesh and heard it sizzle. Despite the unbearable agony, her warrior spirit kept her arm firmly in place. The scorching pain diminished slightly as the flame reached the dirt-ball and shrank to nothing.

Thunder's burn stung unrelentingly for the rest of the day, and whenever her sleeve brushed against it, she nearly shrieked. As the suns went by, the wound slowly healed, and Thunder savored her deed. Conquering her enemy, the pain of her burn, had made her a more courageous warrior.

One night, as Thunder laid out her and Grandfather's blankets for sleeping, she felt a graveness about him.

His eyes met hers. "The settlers have filled the land around us."

"Yes, we knew they would one day," she replied, crawling into her bed.

"And now their sheep and cattle graze everywhere, instead of the animals we hunt for food and hides." Gray Fox continued sadly, "Those animals no longer have enough food, and they are vanishing."

Thunder pulled a blanket over her, worried how they would survive.

Thunder finished the medallion she had made for Golden Eagle. She wore it around her neck, hidden inside her dress. She hoped for a chance to catch him alone and give it to him. She spoke with him whenever they crossed paths, but others grew curious and stared, ruining any opportunity for a private moment.

One evening early in the cold season, Thunder bathed in the stream, trying to ignore the pangs of her empty stomach. While walking the path back to the village, she saw Golden Eagle leaning against a tree just off the trail, Thunder smiled and slowed her pace.

"I have been waiting for you to pass by," he said as he stepped to a log.

"I have hoped for some moons to find you alone," she responded cheerfully.

He sat on the log and patted the spot next to him. She quietly took a seat and waited for him to speak his mind.

"I know I should wait to see how our families arrange things," Golden Eagle began, "but my soul is urging me to speak to you." He smiled and looked into her eyes. "You have charmed me from the moment I first saw you. You are brave, determined, smart, and beautiful."

Thunder realized the intent behind her beloved's words. Her heart pounded in her throat, and her breath grew short.

"Nothing would please me more than to spend the rest of my life with you." His gaze into her eyes deepened. "Thunder, I would like to marry you."

She sat silently, remembering. *First seeing him among the villagers…chasing away my tormentors…teaching me the ways of a warrior…saving my life…sensually caressing me.* Her memories invoked feelings stronger than ever and clearer than the cold waters of a mountain spring. Golden Eagle had come into her life to join with her, to live as one with her in body and spirit. The rightness of this stunned her with the force of its revelation.

She tried to speak, but in her startled elation, she could barely form words. "Yes…yes. Let us marry soon."

Golden Eagle beamed, cupped her face in his hands, and leaned in to kiss her. The moment their lips touched, her heart froze, and just as quickly, it seemed to melt in her chest and spread warmth to every part of her body. They pulled apart from the soft kiss, gazing into each other's eyes.

A sharp sting pierced Thunder's side. *"Aiieeee!"* Then another. She jumped up. "Ants!" Frantically, she reached inside her dress to brush the pests from her body. She looked at Golden Eagle, indignant. "Why did you not tell me we were sitting on an ant-infested log?"

He bolted to his feet and slapped at the ants on himself. "I did not know," he said sheepishly.

She could not help but laugh while swiping the biting ants.

Golden Eagle's smile broadened into a grin, and he stepped over. "Let me help."

As he wiped the ants from Thunder's shoulders and neck, she whispered, "Surely you must know I have always admired you, and how I have hoped for this day. Sharing my life with you will bring me great happiness, and I promise I will always be at your side."

Golden Eagle nodded and gently held her shoulders. "Of course, I would never ask for your hand in marriage without the usual bride price of many fine horses. It would be an insult to your grandfather. Though it may take several moons, my father and I will find a way to make our union honorable and acceptable."

Thunder felt him run his finger along the cord of her hidden medallion. She smiled, reached into her dress, and lifted it over her head. "I made this friendship medallion for you after the raid," she said, "to thank you for saving me." Placing the medallion around his neck, she continued, "With the spirit of a warrior, I give you this token that shows my heart is yours. Regardless of how long it will take, I will stay faithful to you."

They kissed again, and she could feel Golden Eagle's heart beating just as powerfully as her own.

When they parted, Thunder looked up and smiled at Golden Eagle, thinking nothing could come close to describing her joy. He did not break the silence either, but lightly took her hand and walked with her. As they headed back to the village, talking excitedly about their new lives together, the sun moved behind a cloud, fanning vibrant rays across the evening sky.

FIVE

New Mexico Territory, December 1877

The next morning dawned cold; the sky still heavy with the night rain clouds. Thunder awoke to the sound of hooves rumbling toward her lodge. She flung her blanket around her and ducked through the opening. Grandfather stood in front of the lodge, his eyes hard, his hair whipped by the sharp wind. A night guard halted mere paces before him. In the half-light, she instantly recognized Golden Eagle's unique braid decorated with eagle feathers.

"Fifty Bluecoat riders are heading up the mountain from the east!" he reported, his breathing strained.

"Wake everyone," Gray Fox ordered, "and tell the warriors to form a defense line on the east side of camp."

As Golden Eagle rode away, Horse Walker, the western guard, rode up. "A column of Bluecoats is coming from the southwest," he announced, "and another from the northwest."

"How many?"

"Both groups, about a hundred."

Gray Fox ordered Horse Walker to join Golden Eagle and divide the warriors to protect the village from the three-pronged attack.

The darkness had lifted enough for Thunder to see the soldiers. *Every fighter is needed to defeat them.* She hurried into the lodge and returned with her bow and arrows. "I am joining the warriors to fight."

"Not yet, Daughter," Grandfather objected gruffly. His tone would brook no argument. "I want you to stay with me for now."

"Why?"

"I have not yet decided what to do." Through his stoic façade, Thunder could sense tension.

He is right. How can he make a battle plan when he knows so little of our enemy? This is a good chance for me to be at his side, hear the news brought by the warriors, and learn how to lead men in war.

The people quickly took combat positions. Even the women brandished knives, ready to fight to their deaths.

Golden Eagle rode back to Gray Fox, shouting, "We must ride out and attack now, before they use the high ground against us!"

In the gray morning light, Thunder saw the troops encircling the village. They outnumbered the Chiricahua warriors more than five to one. *Golden Eagle is right. We have one last chance to escape and must do it now!*

"No, Golden Eagle," Gray Fox said. "With the whole tribe exposed, many innocent women and children would die."

"They would surely prefer death to surrender," Golden Eagle countered.

"Maybe so," Gray Fox finally replied, "but for their sakes, we must lay down our arms."

Golden Eagle nodded.

Thunder looked up at Grandfather as the heart-wrenching thought of surrender ran through her mind. She would hate to leave home to live far away on a reservation, but the expression of shame in Grandfather's demeanor, caused her to remain silent.

A small group of mounted bluecoats began trotting in from the east.

Grandfather gazed at the horizon, apparently deep in thought. "All of us confined to an unknown place, dependent on our enemies for our very existence." He released a deep sigh. "If we escape, the soldiers would most likely look for us here first. They could divide us in custody, so we need to meet at an isolated location." He called to the warriors to hold their fire and turned back to Golden Eagle. "When we hunted in the Sangre de Cristo Mountains, I saw a good place for a new campsite. Tell the others that whoever escapes should go to the high plateau above Willow Creek."

After Golden Eagle left to spread the word, Grandfather withdrew into the lodge, and when he emerged, a piece of white cloth was tied to his gun barrel.

"Grandfather, did you not vow to never surrender to the white-eyes?"

He nodded and answered quietly, "We must surrender to preserve our lives for now. If we do not, we will starve."

Thunder walked alongside her grandfather as they approached the small group of soldiers, waving the white flag. "I regret what I said to White Cloud winters ago," he told her. "I should not have spoken to him so harshly. He saved your life. Now we are in a similar circumstance, and I must admit that he chose wisely."

Thunder's mind melded with his humiliation and regret, and every step toward surrender intensified their despair.

When they reached the soldiers, two of the men nudged their

horses forward. One was a native scout and the other an older white soldier. He spoke to the scout, who then said in Chiricahua, "Surrender your weapons to Captain Larkin."

Grandfather handed his rifle to the captain, and Thunder gave her bow and arrows to the scout. When asked, Gray Fox told the scout his name.

"Chief Gray Fox, if your people surrender now, no blood will be spilled."

Grandfather stayed silent, waiting for the scout to continue.

"We have set aside land for you less than two days' journey from here. When we reach there, you will be provided food and warm clothing. Also, we will teach all your children as ours are taught."

Grandfather believes the white man's schooling ruins children, Thunder reflected. *He must be recoiling at the thought of the white-eyes poisoning the young ones' minds, but we seem to have little choice.*

"I agree to your terms," Grandfather said, his expression emotionless.

"Chiricahuas…" the captain continued. "I assume you are kin to Geronimo, who is giving us so much trouble. You will be a flight risk with your horses. They will be confiscated."

Though hearing the words through the scout, Gray Fox focused on the captain and took a deep breath. "I have never heard of forfeiting horses as part of a surrender."

Thunder wondered if Grandfather wished he could renege now. At dawn, there had been little chance of the warriors holding the soldiers back while the others got away. But now, with the Bluecoats surrounding the village, they had no chance at all.

"Those are the final terms," the captain said brusquely. "And your people must relinquish their arms now."

Gray Fox turned and ordered the warriors to place their weapons in front of him. Reluctantly, the warriors tossed their clubs, lances, bows, and arrows in a pile. After some discussion with the scout and captain, the warriors finally tossed their guns and ammunition on top.

By then, the Bluecoats had finished rounding up the Apaches' horses and demanded the people start walking. As Thunder ran to the lodge to collect both her and Grandfather's most needed belongings, foot soldiers stomped through the dwellings, driving out the men, women, and children. The soldiers' shouting and commotion sounded to Thunder like a pack of buzzing buffalo flies.

Leaving the wikiup with a bagful of things, she lamented the ugly, muddy mess the whites had made of her cherished village. She returned to Grandfather, and asked, "Where is Stormy?"

"The Bluecoats have herded all our horses far ahead."

The mounted soldiers closed in, forcing the Apaches to walk before them and leave behind any possessions they could not carry. "When will the soldiers return Stormy and the other horses to us?" Thunder asked.

"I doubt you will see Stormy again," Grandfather said. He looked back to the people with concern as they struggled to stay ahead of the soldiers.

Thunder walked alongside Grandfather, enraged. *I would have risked death to keep Stormy.*

The Bluecoats herded the people onward, forcing them to walk throughout the day, all night, and into the next morning. By then, the exhausted children began to lag behind. Seeing this, the younger men dropped their packs to carry them.

It pained Thunder to see even more possessions left behind. Deep in her heart, she knew life would never be the same. Nobody liked reservations, and she would not either. She was woozy from hunger. If she had some food, that would be something. Still, she would have to stand strong for her people. They had given her a warrior's training; for that, she owed them whatever service she could provide. She remembered Grandfather speaking of escape before surrendering. *That may be our only hope.*

At midday, the scout stopped in an open area, ten bowshots to the north of several white men's block-shaped buildings. Off to the east, wisps of smoke and round lodges indicated the presence of other captured tribespeople. Below, to the west, lay a wooded valley and a small stream.

The scout told the Chiricahuas, "This place will be your new home." Without another word, he and the soldiers rode off.

The Apaches began searching the area for branches and leaves to construct new lodges. Late that afternoon, a few soldiers distributed axes and some additional tools. They also brought sacks of cornmeal and other foodstuffs to the tired, hungry Apaches. Thunder met Young Falcon in the food line and was delighted to learn her friend kept Grandfather's shirt with her. Thunder took it for safekeeping.

Using the white men's tools, the Apaches finished the new village in a couple of days. At dawn on the third day of captivity, mounted soldiers stormed the Apache settlement. Pointing their rifles at the younger braves, they motioned for them to move away from the others. Thunder overheard the scout tell Grandfather, "…laborers to build a new fort." The soldiers set apart Golden Eagle and twelve other braves, including Silver Leaf and Firemaker.

Thunder felt sure she would not see Golden Eagle for a long time, maybe never. Distraught and afraid this might be her only chance to say goodbye, she ran to the group of braves and embraced her love. Holding him tightly, she whispered, "I love you."

A soldier yelled and waved his gun as he steered his horse to run her out.

"I love you too." Golden Eagle held her in front of him, looking her in the eyes. "Keep yourself safe."

The soldier reached them, barking unintelligibly, and pointed his rifle at Thunder. "I will stay true to you, Golden Eagle, I promise," she said as tears welled in her eyes. She turned, slipped through the braves, and back to Grandfather.

For much of the day, Golden Eagle and the other warriors walked briskly ahead of the mounted soldiers on a southeastward trail. Late in the afternoon, they came to the building site of the new adobe fort. The soldiers chained Golden Eagle, Crossing Wolf, and Two Feathers together at the ankles. They led the Apaches to where men already toiled, mixing water, sand, straw, and clay into a muddy pile. The soldiers motioned to the Apaches to join in shoveling the mud into boxes. Another group upended the boxes and laid out the bricks to dry.

At night—still chained—they made a campfire, and a soldier came to them, handing out bowls of soup. Crossing Wolf took a bowl and swirled it around. He looked at the soup closely, took a sip, then spat. "Ground ears of corn and bones boiled in water. Dogs eat better than this!"

Golden Eagle had no appetite. He sat glumly by the fire. Being separated from Thunder made him heartsick. He took out the medallion she had given him and examined it closely in the firelight. Within the round patch of stitched buckskin, Thunder had worked the beads into a striking design of the radiant Morning Star. *How beautiful. Just like her.* Thankful for the affectionate gift, he vowed to do everything in his power to return to her soon.

Late that night, Thunder recalled the rumor spreading earlier in the day. *Tomorrow, the soldiers will take females under sixteen, not expecting or with children, to a school a day's ride away.* Throughout the night, thoughts of leaving Grandfather and her people filled her with despondency. Anxious for Golden Eagle and worried she might never see him again, she barely slept.

At dawn, Thunder stepped outside the lodge, where ten armed soldiers confronted her. They motioned for her to climb into a buckboard wagon with five other girls, all under eleven winters. Grandfather stood a few paces away, gravely watching the scene.

Thunder thought of the shirt she had intended to finish for him. Though she still wished to make designs for the sleeves, she had to give it to him now. Before the soldiers could object, she bolted back into the lodge, rummaged through her things, and pulled it out. She stepped back outside, holding the folded shirt. "I made this for you, Grandfather."

Gray Fox lifted the shirt by the top of the sleeves to inspect it. An intricate array of decorative beads and quills covered the cream-colored leather. "These are the best-crafted decorations I have ever seen," he said, smiling sadly. "Thank you, Daughter. I will wear it until you return." He grasped her shoulders as three soldiers rapidly approached them. "You must go now, child. I wish you well."

Thunder smiled with watery eyes at the compliment and hugged Grandfather one last time, savoring the familiar smell of tobacco on his robe. As she released the embrace, she felt her bracelet—her mother's gift—sliding down her forearm. She removed the turquoise keepsake and gave it to him.

"I am sure this will be safest with you," she said. "I hope I will not be kept long." With a final look, Thunder turned and stoically walked away.

As she approached the buckboard wagon, Thunder saw a girl was already chained to a metal ring at the back. The soldiers chained the other girls to one another at the wrist. Thunder boarded, and the oldest soldier, his face pitted by pox, grabbed her wrist to chain her to Rolling Cloud. Fear radiated from the girl's deep brown eyes.

Nauseated by the stench wafting from the ugly soldier, Thunder told Rolling Cloud, "He reeks even worse than the spray of a polecat."

Rolling Cloud's face lit up. She giggled and said, "That is a good name for him."

Polecat barked something, and Thunder assumed he wanted them to stay quiet. Giving Thunder a sly grin, he yanked her wrist roughly and enclosed it in a metal bracelet attached to the chain. He twisted a strange twig-like piece of metal into its clasp, which clicked somewhere inside and stayed closed. Alarm stirred within Thunder followed by a sinking feeling in the pit of her stomach.

After boarding the wagon, Polecat slapped the reins on the horses' backs. The buckboard rolled ahead, and Thunder watched her grandfather slowly disappear from sight.

Before long, Polecat looked back at Thunder and spouted gibberish, seeming to scoff at her with his callous, grating voice. He looked only at her, never at the other girls, and she knew he wanted to harm her.

She told the girls, "If there is trouble, I am counting on all of you to do whatever it takes to fight."

"How will we fight in chains?" Rolling Cloud asked.

"The girls near the back of the wagon will not fight," Thunder responded, "but only stretch their arms to give the rest of us slack.

Those in the middle can attack his side closest to the back of the wagon while you and I attack his other side."

She examined her enemy. She guessed him to have about thirty-five winters, and twice her weight.

A couple of soldiers came galloping toward them on the barely used trail. They swung their right hands up to their foreheads as they passed, and Polecat did the same.

They traveled a long distance in the warm sun. Polecat kept looking back at her, laughing and rasping unintelligibly. A horse-drawn wagon passed them carrying five settlers of various ages who seemed to take little notice of their surroundings. Thunder guessed them to be a family. *They do not know their luck in having one another.*

At midday, Polecat steered the wagon across a tree-lined stream and pulled the horses to a stop two bowshots off the trail. He dismounted and tied the horses to a sapling. While walking back to the wagon, he pulled the metal twig out of his pocket. He waved his finger to all the girls before pointing to the creek.

Nobody was in sight, and Polecat stood a few paces from the buckboard, grinning.

"His offer for us to drink at the stream must be a ruse," Thunder told the girls. "There are six of us. Together, we will attack him when I give the war cry. Grab whatever limb you are closest to, and once we have held him back, I will take the gun."

Thunder waited for all the girls to hop from the wagon before she, too, jumped down.

Suddenly Polecat took two giant steps and slammed his body into Thunder's back, pinning her against the buckboard. She let out an ear-piercing shriek, and the girls lunged for his limbs. Thunder flung her arms back, hoping to grasp either a piece of him or—better yet—the gun. Polecat twisted sharply and broke his right arm loose from Rolling Cloud's grip. Thunder felt the cold muzzle of his pistol against her head.

"Stop!" she cried to the girls.

In the silence, she heard only Polecat's ragged breathing and her own thrashing heartbeat.

Using his left hand, Polecat took Thunder's wrist and set it on the buckboard. He rammed the metal twig into the bracelet and twisted it open, then grabbed her upper arm and led her away, keeping his pistol to her head.

The young girls chained to the wagon screamed. Polecat spun his head toward them and hollered, "Shadap!" But the girls shrieked even louder. For a split moment, he seemed puzzled, as if he had not expected the screaming. Turning his gaze between Thunder and the other girls, he grated out gibberish so intensely that his spittle hit her face. His fleshy, pitted cheeks shook as his lips moved.

Thunder twisted her head and bit hard into the man's shirt at the side of his chest, hoping to find his flesh. He cried out and smacked the back of her head with the pistol. Knocked dizzy by the blow, she lost her bite and tried to keep her balance. Releasing her arm, he pulled a stained white cloth from his reeking shirt and stuffed it into her mouth. It tasted repulsive, nearly making her vomit. She kicked at his feet and knees as he dragged her to a nearby thicket. Beyond the sight of the screaming girls, the enraged Polecat whacked her harder with the gun and hollered, "Staup it!"

Thunder almost fell unconscious from the impact; she put her entire focus into collecting her wits. Polecat pressed the gun to the back of her head, behind her ear. She twisted and kicked at him even harder, fully aware he could kill her at any moment. He pulled a short rope from his pocket and tried to whip it around her wrist.

Suddenly, a man shouted from several paces away. A broad-shouldered young soldier rode in with pistol drawn. Never in her life had Thunder seen a man so muscular. As the two soldiers yelled at each other, Polecat's gun shook against her skull. She had one chance to survive—*hit the gun and fight to kill!*

The stranger dismounted, and when he advanced to within an arm's length of Polecat, Thunder slammed her hand upward into the pistol. The gun fired, and a bullet ripped painfully through the upper edge of her ear. Whipping up her hands, she clawed at his eyes in a mad flurry. The other soldier clamped his arms around Polecat's chest and wrestled him to the ground.

While backing away to avoid any stray bullets, Thunder took the cloth from her mouth and stuffed it in her pocket. A piercing sting burned the top of her ear as blood ran down and dripped on her shoulder. *I will deal with that after I finish with Polecat.* Each man strained, reaching and grabbing with his left hand at the pistol in the other's right. The newcomer's hat fell off, revealing hair as white as a new snowfall. Dirt and dust billowed around the soldiers, obscuring them from Thunder's sight. Breaking his right hand free, Snow threw his own pistol two paces away from the fight and twenty-five paces from Thunder. She sprinted for the gun as the white-haired soldier whisked dirt in Polecat's face and wrenched his pistol away. She was only ten paces from the pistol when Snow rolled over, grabbed his own pistol, and rose to his knees with a gun in each hand.

Still running at full speed, Thunder looked to Polecat lying on the ground, rubbing his eyes. She veered toward him, jumped high, and brought her feet together. The dazed man turned his head, just as she rammed her heels into his left ear and jaw. She knelt and spun around to take his eyes out, but a sudden yank at her hair pulled her up and back. The end of Snow's pistol pressed hard between her shoulder blades. His grip on her hair and the barrel of the gun lifted her up, and she had to arch her back to keep her feet on the ground.

He pulled her away from Polecat, and she stumbled backward to keep pace. Snow stopped; the hard-downward pull on her hair and the immovable gun at her back forced her face toward the sun. *He is even stronger than he looks! Why does he not let me fight it out with Polecat?*

Snow shouted at Polecat. Thunder strained her eyes downward, over her cheeks, to see the man walk toward the wagon. The pressure of Snow's gun forced her to follow Polecat.

Grumbling, Polecat took a chain from the front of the buckboard and latched it on the opposite side of the wagon from the girls, then backed away.

Snow pushed her forward until they reached the chain, close enough for the girls to reach Snow. Rolling Cloud threw her a questioning look. *Our last chance to fight,* Thunder thought. *But if I order an attack, some of us might get killed.* The pistol pushed harder into her back, and Snow spoke sternly. Thunder hesitated, wishing she could understand him. *If I let him rechain me, I will again be defenseless. Yet I must take the chance and submit.* She put her left wrist on the metal and the man let go of her hair and latched the chain. He pulled out the twig and, as he moved away, so did the gun.

Snow glanced at Polecat, stared sidelong at Thunder, shook his head, and sighed. While letting out a long breath, he kicked the dirt. Snow seemed to be dazed and lost, almost as if she had disappointed him. He motioned Thunder and the other girls to board the wagon.

Tying his own horse's reins to the buckboard, Snow called to Polecat, who untied the other horses from the small tree. Both men boarded the wagon, Snow pointing a gun at Polecat, who took the reins and hollered to the horses. As the buckboard moved forward, Thunder watched Polecat sitting hunched over, his face and ear swollen. Snow handed him a white cloth, and he wiped around his bleeding eye.

Looking on with satisfaction, Thunder saw she had furrowed a deep gash from his left eye to his ear and torn his upper eyelid. *I hope his eye is punctured too. That would serve him right.* She crawled to little more than an arm's length away from Polecat. *I might be able to kill him yet.* But the chain tightened before she could reach him.

Rolling Cloud slid close to her. "Your ear is bleeding."

Thunder reached into her pocket and brought out the foul piece of cloth from Polecat. Her friend took it and wiped the blood off her neck and shoulder.

"Where did the young soldier come from?" Thunder asked.

"I do not know," Rolling Cloud said, shaking her head. "We were screaming when he arrived and looked at us. When we pointed at the trampled trail you had made, he followed it and found you."

Thunder scanned the faces of the other girls. Some had fewer winters than she'd had when she left the White Mountain village. *They must all be frightened.*

"The danger has passed," she told them. "Your screams saved me from death—or worse." While the wagon bounced along, she answered their questions and calmed their fears. Before long, they grew quiet.

By the time the sun dipped low in the west, a massive square adobe structure came into view. It had a pointed top, like an arrowhead aimed at the sky. Some smaller buildings surrounded it. Ten bowshots beyond those lay a fort, enclosed by a wall. The uselessly huge buildings of the whites amazed Thunder, but the fort and so many soldiers left her uneasy.

Polecat stopped the horses in front of the big structure. A woman in a long brown dress approached the wagon, her black hair bundled on her head. She spoke to the men, then went to a small building nearby. After a few moments she emerged, carrying a piece of cloth and a jar. She returned to Snow, and he gave her the twig-like piece of metal. Thunder saw that the apple-cheeked woman wore a smile, a real one. She turned to the girls and introduced herself in Spanish. "My name is Miss Ortega. I am a teacher and occasionally help the injured."

Thunder's people knew Spanish from generations of trading with the Mexicans. Hearing the familiar words pleased her.

Holding up the piece of cloth, the woman looked at Thunder and said, "Let me treat your wound."

Thunder moved to the side of the buckboard, where Miss Ortega closely examined her ear, then applied salve and a bandage. "I'm afraid there is nothing I can do for the bumps on your head," she said as she finished. She unchained the girls, who happily jumped from the wagon, finally free from the soldiers. Snow nodded, Polecat slapped the horses with the reins, and the buckboard lumbered away toward the fort.

Miss Ortega asked the girls to follow her, then walked to the largest building. She took a burning lantern from a hook on the wall and led them through an open door into a small, empty room. "This is where you will spend the night," Miss Ortega said softly. "I will come for you in the morning." She turned and left the room, taking the lantern. The door closed behind her, plunging the Apaches into absolute darkness.

Several of the girls began to chatter. "Quiet!" Thunder ordered. "They have trapped us here, but we must try to escape." She sat in the dark for a few moments, picturing the room surrounding her. She remembered seeing no possible exit other than the door. Slowly, Thunder felt her way along a wall to the door. She pushed and pulled with all her strength, but it did not budge.

She crept back to the girls. "No way out," she told them. "We must show these people that we are strong and without fear. Rest now, for strength, and let tomorrow bring what it will. We will face it as Apaches."

Even as Thunder said the words, she knew she meant them largely for herself. She lay down and took a deep breath. A throb in her ear brought her thoughts back to Polecat, but she shoved the image from her mind.

As if by habit, Thunder's wandering thoughts landed on Golden Eagle, which brought sharp tears to her eyes. She never could have faced him again if Polecat had succeeded in his vicious assault on her. He had tried to take from her what she meant to give Golden Eagle. Rage filled her mind, and her purpose was set. Somehow, she would find a way to kill Polecat.

SIX

New Mexico Territory, December 1877

Thunder awoke to Miss Ortega opening the door. She clapped her hands loudly and said, "Come with me."

Following Miss Ortega and the other girls outside, Thunder squinted in the intense sunlight. A curved path led them back into the building through another entrance, and they walked down a dimly lit passageway. The strong odor of many unwashed bodies living too close together wafted over the girls and made Thunder slightly sick to her stomach.

They reached a wooden bench along the walkway with an open door on the opposite side. Miss Ortega pointed to the bench and told Thunder, "Sit here. I will be back after I take these younger girls to others their age." She told the girls to follow her and left.

Thunder sat primly on the hard bench, looking into the small square room. Inside, an old white-skinned woman sat behind a waist-high block of smooth wood. Dressed like Miss Ortega, the old woman faced a girl who sat with her head bowed. The girl wore settlers' clothing, yet her skin was not white but golden brown, like Thunder's. Thunder narrowed her eyes in discomfort. She would never cower in such a way.

Miss Ortega returned, called the girl from the room, and stopped near Thunder as the girl walked away.

Thunder asked, "When will my younger friends come back?"

"You will not see them often, since the younger girls stay in another building. Don't worry; I teach there. I will tell you if any of them has a problem." Miss Ortega gestured to the doorway. "Principal Smith will see you now." Thunder entered the room and remained standing, Miss Ortega behind her.

The tiny woman had a small round, red-veined face. Her bright eyes did not smile when the rest of her face did. She moved her lips, speaking a string of words Thunder could not comprehend.

Beady little rat eyes, Thunder thought, immediately distrusting this Principal Smith. Her warrior's instincts alerted as if by an enemy, she made no move.

The woman uttered more gibberish. Thunder tried to force an unfriendly smile like the principal's but could not do it. Such a false expression would surely crack her face.

Seemingly unperturbed, Principal Smith waved her hand at Miss Ortega.

"Is this your first time at a school?" the younger teacher asked.

"Yes," Thunder said. After a short question-and-answer session translated by Miss Ortega, the principal seemed satisfied. Finally, Miss Ortega said, "Principal Smith has given you the name Harriet, and you are expected to answer to it, or be punished. Also, from this point on, you are expected to speak only English at the school."

Thunder had no intention of abiding by these absurd demands, but she nodded out of respect for Miss Ortega.

The principal raised a cone-shaped metal object and shook it, making a loud tinkling sound. Two girls of about Thunder's age entered, brown-skinned like her. Their dark braids bounced against their settlers' dresses as they stepped to the center of the room. They stopped in front of the desk and stood rigidly. After an exchange with Principal Smith, they led Thunder from the room and down a long, white-walled passageway. Paintings of white people in white gowns lined the walls. Thunder studied the lifeless, soulless images and wondered who they were.

Both girls giggled. "People of God," the taller girl whispered in Spanish, as if she had read Thunder's mind. "I am Helen," she said, then pointed to the girl walking with them. "And she is Teresa."

When Teresa looked at her bandaged ear, Thunder squelched the implied question. "An accident in my village yesterday," she said, and quickly changed the subject. "Why did Principal Smith give me a different name?"

"She gave all of us settlers' names when we arrived here," Teresa said. "You must answer to Harriet."

"I will not. Grandfather named me Talks Like Thunder."

"I know it will be difficult, Talks Like Thunder," Teresa replied, empathy in her voice. "You will be punished unless you pretend your name is Harriet."

"I have no respect for this woman and will not answer to a foreign name."

"For your sake," Helen said, "I hope you will." She smiled slyly. "We will call you Talks Like Thunder when we're away from the teachers."

Thunder did not answer, offended by Principal Smith's demand.

Her tribal elders had spoken truly when they warned her that white-eyes had cold hearts. "*Ar-Arret,*" she mumbled to herself, annoyed she could not even pronounce the word.

Upon reaching the end of the narrow passageway, Helen opened two big doors. "This room is called the *dormitory.*"

Hearing the English word, Thunder repeated *dormitory* in her mind.

They entered the large room with two rows of low, flat, rectangular objects. In the center of the room stood a big metal barrel as tall as Thunder. The barrel bulged in the middle, and a black pipe extended from its top up to the roof.

Seeing the uncomprehending look on Thunder's face, Teresa laughed. "This is where we sleep."

"Sleep?" Thunder cried out, amazed. "On these things, off the ground?"

"They're called *beds,*" Helen said. "Yours is here, next to the door; mine is on the other side of you."

Thunder echoed *beds* to herself. Helen held out a settler's dress. "Take off your buckskin and moccasins and put this on."

"Do as you wish with it!" Thunder snapped. "I will not wear settlers' clothing."

"Like you, all of us girls have been captured and taken from our people. The teachers insist we all wear the clothing of their people." Helen put her hand on Thunder's shoulder. "Please wear the dress. It will make your life much easier here. Believe me."

Seeing the pleading look in Helen's eyes, Thunder grudgingly relented. After removing her moccasins, she pulled off her clothing and slipped on the nearly weightless cloth dress. It made her feel almost naked. "And what do they give us to put on our feet?"

Helen looked at her own bare feet. "As you can see, nothing."

The girls took Thunder outside and into a small structure behind the school. Shiny metallic wash tubs hung on every wall, and beneath them sat many crude log benches.

"This is our *bath house* and where we wash our clothes," Teresa explained.

Thunder stepped out and looked at the adobe buildings surrounding her. "When did the white-eyes make this village?"

"The Mexicans built it as a place of worship many years ago," Helen answered. "When they abandoned it, the white-eyes made it our school."

"And there is our *privy*," Teresa added, pointing to a smaller hut. Sensing Thunder's confusion, she squatted and pretended to wipe herself.

Thunder burst out laughing at the thought of anyone relieving herself indoors. *How stinky it must be*, she thought, and laughed even louder.

Helen and Teresa sat Thunder on a bench and went to work combing her hair. She grimaced as the comb tore at her scalp.

"Your hair is too thick," Helen said. "Miss Lynch, the head teacher, will not let you run around looking like a haystack. We're going to braid it."

"No! I never braid my hair."

"Just sit still," Helen said sternly. "We know the rules, and we're trying to help you avoid punishments."

"I am not afraid of these old ladies." Thunder tried to stand, but both the girls pushed her down.

"You should know, Thunder, you will never get the best of the teachers," Teresa advised. "They can always get help from the Army, who can send the unruly to a place so far away that they can never return."

Thunder sat still for a moment as the truth of her new reality broke over her. She had to follow the senseless rules or never see her people again. "Why did Principal Smith tell me to speak only English? Is Miss Lynch making these stupid rules?"

"No," Teresa answered. "Principal Smith makes the rules, and Miss Lynch enforces them."

"If I do not know the language, how can they expect me to speak it?"

"Say nothing within hearing of the teachers until you learn it," Helen said.

After finishing with Thunder's braids, Helen gave her a piece of silver glass. "This is called a *mirror*. Take a look."

When Thunder saw her reflection, she swore under her breath, horrified. She hated the braids forced upon her as if she had never trained as a warrior. "Take them out!"

"You had better keep the braids, or you'll end up in the punishment hut," Helen said.

"What is that?"

"It is about the size of the privy, only it's made so heavily that no one can get out."

"What would I do there?"

"Nothing. It's dark, and you have no food or water until the teachers decide to let you out. Nothing distracts you from becoming dreadfully homesick. You will be miserable."

A sudden clanging noise nearby caused Thunder to jump up and look about. Both girls laughed, and Teresa pointed to a dome-shaped metal object swiveling under a peaked roof. "It is called a *bell*. It tells us when it's time for different activities." She grabbed Thunder's arm. "Now it's time to eat." The girls led her to the eating room. Once again, Thunder was awed by the sheer size of the room and by the many girls sitting on benches throughout it.

"The big slabs of wood with bowls and plates are called *tables*," Teresa told her.

As they walked toward a half-occupied table, Helen whispered in her ear, "The tall girl sitting at the end of the table is Dorothy. Watch out for her." The girls sat, with Thunder between Helen and Dorothy.

Wheezing came from Dorothy's bent nose as she took a plate from a stack, onto which she ladled brown goo from a large bowl. Whining unintelligibly, she handed the dish to the girl to her right. That girl passed it on to the next girl, and the dish went around the table. The annoying sound of Dorothy's singsong voice made Thunder instantly dislike her.

Finally, Dorothy served herself a full plate, nearly emptying the large bowl, before scooping the last of the goo, only a half portion, onto Thunder's plate. She stared at the small heap of muck, then at Dorothy. *She must know I did not eat when they brought me here yesterday. She gave me a half serving on purpose.* Although the rank-smelling mess nauseated her, she raised a spoonful to take a bite out of sheer hunger. Dorothy's hand whipped across the table and slapped hers. Before she could retaliate, Helen grabbed her hand and murmured in Spanish, "Stand to say grace." As they rose, Helen whispered, "Miss Lynch saw you take food from your plate before grace. She may come to you. Do not fight her."

Just then, Thunder noticed a fat woman stroll across the room so quietly, it seemed Apaches had trained her. *She must be Miss Lynch.* Watching the others through half-open eyes, Thunder put her hands together as they did. While the group recited a prayer, Thunder moved her lips silently, trying to retain some of the strange words. If saying these words meant she could eat, she intended to learn them quickly.

When the prayer finished, the woman spun about on one heel and walked toward Thunder. Her face had perfectly regular features, and she would have been pretty except for the coldness in her eyes. She stopped directly in front of Thunder, pointing at her. In a disapproving tone, she spewed forth a string of babble.

Thunder took Miss Lynch's pointing hand, as she had seen the soldiers do, and shook it politely. She hastily returned to her seat. Looking confused, Miss Lynch turned and walked to the far end of the room where she stood and watched them.

Thunder raised a spoonful of the slime to her lips and took a mouthful. It tasted rotten. She instantly spat it out. Hissing erupted from the others at her table. The looks on their faces—some astonished, many worried, a few wincing—told Thunder she had made a big mistake.

Miss Lynch yelled, "Harriet!" She beckoned to Thunder with her long, white index finger. Muscles taut, Thunder rose, and walked past the chortling Dorothy, to the woman who erupted into a screaming tirade.

Thunder could not understand Miss Lynch, but the animosity in the teacher's voice warned her to remain standing. She clamped her mouth tightly shut and stood ramrod straight, trying to hold back her rage.

The sound of Dorothy's continued snickering infuriated her. *She will pay for this*, Thunder promised herself. *One way or another, I will make Dorothy pay!* After Miss Lynch stopped speaking, Thunder started back to the eating table. But a hand clamped onto her elbow, and Miss Lynch steered her outside to the punishment hut. The boards of the tiny, dilapidated structure were warped and split from the desert sun.

As Thunder stepped inside, she saw the old planks were three layers thick. *Helen was right. There is no breaking out of here.* The door closed, leaving the hut dark except for chinks and slivers of light shining through the roof, walls, and floor. Unable to lie down or even move much, Thunder resigned herself to sitting on the floor or standing. She tried to daydream about her good times with Golden Eagle and their future together. Soon, however, the dreams turned into melancholy as she began to worry about him working under the white-eyes at the faraway fort. *Will the soldiers treat him well? Will he get the same bad food as here, or even worse?* The day wore on, and a terrible feeling of loneliness washed over her, as she cried, missing her people.

Late that afternoon, when Miss Lynch let Thunder out, a cold breeze hit her. She saw the skyline filling with clouds. *A snowstorm is brewing.* As she joined the others near the eating room, Helen pulled her aside. "I am so glad she let you out of there. But never spit out your food—it's not allowed."

"Swallowing even one mouthful of that rotten food would make me sick."

"You may become ill at first, but you'll get used to it," Helen said. "And you must pretend to respect Miss Lynch, even if you don't."

"I will not cower in front of her. Besides, she has already had the satisfaction of punishing me."

Helen shrugged. "Proud, aren't you? Well, just wait. Miss Lynch has a heavy hand, and she will crush your pride, just as she's done with all the rest of us." The bell rang again, and the girls filed in for supper.

The meal passed without incident. Thunder forced the same tasteless muck into her mouth and washed it down with a cup of water. She beseeched the spirits to help her hold the foul-tasting mess in her stomach.

The bell rang again, and all the girls rose. Helen grabbed Thunder's arm and whispered, "Come with us." Joining the swarm of girls, they exited the room of terrible food.

They went to the dormitory, where Helen walked up to the metal barrel. "This is called a *pot-bellied stove*," she told Thunder as she opened a door on the side of the barrel. Picking up some logs cut to arm's length, she threw them into the stove. Next to the stove lay a big pile of heavy sticks and bundles of tinder tied with string.

Suddenly, a girl Thunder had not seen before slipped an apple into Thunder's pocket, then moved away before she could thank her. *What a strange place. Why are some people so cruel and others so kind?*

Again, the bell rang, and Miss Lynch entered the room and clapped her hands. They all knelt for evening prayers. When the long recitation ended, the bell rang again, and the girls began to change into sleeping clothes.

As Thunder removed her dress, she felt eyes watching her. She glanced up to see Miss Lynch coming toward her, flapping her arms and shrieking like a hawk. The woman picked up a long-sleeved nightshirt and pulled it over Thunder's head, motioning for her to undress beneath it. Puzzled and irritated, she let her dress fall to the floor. *How could the sight of my body offend these crazy people?*

Dorothy sneered something in English. Thunder cut her eyes in the girl's direction as Dorothy stared back and stuck out her tongue. Thunder recognized the vile nature of Dorothy and her friends. To win the teachers' favor, they dishonored and stood against everything their elders had taught them. She returned Dorothy's taunt with an expression of disgust.

When another bell rang, all the girls went to their cots and stood rigidly.

Bells, bells, Thunder fumed. *Bells to eat, bells to stop eating, bells to pray, bells to sleep...* She wondered if they would ring a bell for her to relieve herself. If so, she hoped it would ring soon. Now she actually looked forward to going to the little privy out back.

When Miss Lynch seemed content with their obedience, the girls filed outside in silence. A cold wind stung Thunder's exposed skin, and small snowflakes flew in the wind. After a visit to the privy and a quick splash of cold water, the girls returned to the dormitory and got in bed.

After Miss Lynch closed the door, Thunder asked Helen, "What did Dorothy say to me?"

"Just ignore it, Thunder," Helen whispered harshly.

"No, what did she say?"

"She called you 'rag ear.'"

"She will not get away with it," Thunder said loudly enough for all to hear.

Thunder rolled over, trying to ignore the sag of the thin straw bag and the creaking of the supporting ropes. Metal beds lined the dirty white walls, and the room had an unpleasant odor. She thought she could feel the presence of a malevolent spirit and feared it might pounce on her the moment she closed her eyes. Still, she tried to sleep, but the bed squeaked every time she moved. She tossed and turned for most of the night until, exasperated, she slipped off the bed and curled up beneath it.

She awoke in semi-darkness, not remembering where she was until the clicking of shoes forced her mind into keen awareness. From the floor, she could see exposed, white undergarments, then recognized the woman's grumbling—Miss Lynch. She screamed a steady stream of gibberish as her hand reached under the bed. Thunder felt the cold grip on her wrist and knew she was in trouble. She tried to retreat deeper into the darkness, before remembering Helen saying, *Do not fight her.*

Miss Lynch pulled her up from under the bed and beat her about her head and arms with a stick. Thunder stepped back, but the woman followed closely. Her fleshy, heavy-lidded eyes and her deep, rapid breathing made her seem like an evil spirit in a nightmare. *What have I done to make her so angry?* Thunder backed through the double doors.

Another blow split her lip, and blood spurted onto Miss Lynch's brown sleeve, causing the woman to screech like an enraged vulture. Miss Lynch returned to swinging the stick as Thunder held her arms in front of her face to block the assault. Rage suddenly erupted from the depths of Thunder's being. She clenched her right hand into a fist and slammed it into Miss Lynch's nose. The woman's head flung back from the blow, then slowly wobbled back upright. Terror flashed across her face, her mouth agape, blood streaming from both nostrils.

Thunder shook with fury. *She knows if she hits me with that stick one more time, I will kill her.*

Miss Lynch took a cloth from her pocket and wiped off the blood. A flutter in her eyes told Thunder that she had a harsher punishment in mind. Thunder unclenched her fists. *For the sake of returning to my people, I must hold back and let her have her way.*

Miss Lynch grabbed her by the hair and dragged her outside into the now-fierce snowstorm. Away from the buildings, the woman stopped and forced her to kneel in the ankle-deep snow. Behind Thunder, the wake-up bell sounded. Instinctively, she turned her head toward the noise, but Miss Lynch rapped her firmly with her stick. Then, she pressed the stick down on Thunder's shoulder in a clear warning not to move. A moment later, she walked away.

Thunder stayed put while the predawn gloom lightened into the gray of an overcast sky. As the day wore on, the wind and snow whipped around her bare arms and legs. Rigorous warrior training had taught her to use her inner nature to fend off the nearly unbearable cold. She fought against the freezing, cramping pain by calling up the power within herself to endure. Regardless, her body neared its limits.

Thunder plotted ways to take revenge on Miss Lynch, but Teresa was right; there was no way to get even. Thoughts of running away stampeded through her mind. *Return to Grandfather and my people...but if the teachers report me missing, soldiers will find me and bring me back for more punishment.* She recalled her grandfather's words: "Whoever escapes should go to the high plateau above Willow Creek." She did not know where Willow Creek was or whether her people would try to escape. But she knew she could not abandon her grandfather, let alone the rest of her people. While they remained in captivity, she would not forsake them.

By late afternoon, the snow had drifted over Thunder's legs. Her feet, no longer cold, now burned with searing-hot pain. Just before dark, Miss Ortega and a taller woman came to Thunder. They shook their heads, conversing quietly. Then, very gently, they picked her up and carried her inside, into a small room. While the taller woman poured water into a bowl, Miss Ortega helped Thunder into a clean nightdress. She seated her in a chair and said, "Miss Lorence is my aide. We will need to warm your feet."

Miss Ortega's kind voice quelled Thunder's wariness. The women placed the bowl of water on the floor in front of her. They raised her feet and lowered them into the bowl. She cringed from the sting of the water but stayed silent.

"You poor little thing," Miss Ortega whispered. Then she cautioned, "Do not tell anyone I spoke with you in Spanish, or we will be punished."

Later, Miss Ortega lifted Thunder's feet from the water. The two small toes on her left foot had swollen and turned deep red. After gently dabbing them dry with a thick cloth, Miss Ortega carefully applied a sweet-smelling balm. She and Miss Lorence put her into a bed and covered her with a heavy blanket.

Miss Ortega took two folded tortillas from her pocket and set them into Thunder's hand. She leaned down until her lips almost touched Thunder's ear, and whispered, "Sleep in the bed, not under it."

SEVEN

New Mexico Territory, December 1877

After a third night in the infirmary, Miss Lorence brought Thunder breakfast. When she finished eating, Miss Ortega removed the bandage from her ear. "It has healed quite well and should be fine, but be careful not to bump it when bathing and resting." She knelt, lifted Thunder's feet to a footstool, and examined her shriveled blue toes. She asked Thunder if she could walk, and as she hobbled around the room, the bell clanged.

"It would be best for you to start your classes today," Miss Ortega said. "Go to the eating room. Miss Graves will take the students to your classroom. However, I am still concerned about your toes. Return here in three days, so I can take another look at them."

On the way to the eating room, Thunder saw teachers leading

students to different buildings. A bulky woman led a group of students, including Helen and Teresa. Trotting to catch up, Thunder blocked the pain in her toes by focusing on the teachers.

Miss Graves dressed like all the others, their clothing exposing only little round faces and short stubby fingers. *Surely, they committed crimes and now work here as punishment. Why else would they have such hateful attitudes?* Thunder checked their noses and saw they had not been slit. *So*, she guessed, *they have not committed adultery.* Their misdeeds *must* have had something to do with men, though, since not one of them had a husband.

She caught up to the group as they entered a smaller building with a wooden floor. More floors, more teachers, and more of everything she hated. *Do these people never want to see Father Sun or Moon Maiden? Do they never want to feel the glory of a cool rain or the caress of an autumn breeze? Do the whites like anything?*

A pot-bellied stove occupied the center of the room. Small tables in neat rows faced a large wooden table where Miss Graves sat, frowning. Copying the others, Thunder seated herself on a little bench next to one of the small tables. She looked up and spied a small field mouse crawling along the metal stovepipe. Grinning, she watched the mouse jump onto a support beam, then scurry up and down the beam's length. She wondered if the mouse too sought a way out of this white man's world.

Crack!

Thunder dropped to the floor and took cover under her table. She lay like a frightened rabbit, praying a bullet would not find her. To her surprise, the students laughed as if nothing had gone wrong. Then she realized Miss Graves had merely rapped a piece of wood against her desktop.

"Harriet!" The sharpness of Miss Graves' voice and the classmates' laughter embarrassed Thunder. She returned to her seat and sat stiffly, determined not to move until class ended. While the incomprehensible babble droned on, Thunder tried to listen but could only think how vulnerable she was not knowing the whites' language. *If I can learn English, I will more likely survive this place and return to Grandfather.*

Another bell rang, and Miss Graves stopped speaking. As the students rose from their desks, Thunder asked Helen, "What are we doing now?"

"It's our morning playtime," Helen answered. "The teachers call it *recess*."

The students went outdoors, and Thunder walked to the middle of the play yard. Standing on her good foot, she watched the others play a game called *tag*. Helen was tagged, then ran until she touched Dorothy, who started for Thunder. She began to jog away. *I cannot run well, but I can put a stop to her bullying. The teachers will punish me, but it will be worth the pain.* As Dorothy came closer, Thunder darted her eyes about, seeing no teachers. Just as Dorothy tagged her, Thunder tagged her back by sinking a hard-fisted blow to her stomach, then shoved her down. The girl fell screaming, her knees and hands spurting blood onto the sharp gravel.

Miss Graves and Miss Lynch waddled across the play yard like two plump squawking ducks. Miss Lynch steered Dorothy, blubbering and dripping blood, in the opposite direction from the classroom. *Probably going to the infirmary*, Thunder thought cheerfully.

Miss Graves took Thunder back into the classroom. There, she drew a circle on the blackboard at the level of Thunder's forehead. She grabbed Thunder's braids, pulled her upward until she stood on her toes, and walked her to the blackboard. Still holding the braids tightly, the teacher pushed Thunder's nose against the circle. She stayed on her toes for a moment, but the pain of her injured toes caused her to lower her heels and stand flatfooted. Miss Graves took her by her good ear and raised her to the same spot, an obvious command to stay put. Moments later, Thunder flushed with embarrassment as the students passed through the doorway, whispering and pointing at her.

The students settled in at their desks, and Miss Graves began speaking again. Before long, the searing pain radiating from Thunder's toes became almost unbearable. To block the pain, she recalled sending Dorothy to the infirmary and smiled.

When the class went to the noon meal, Miss Graves took Thunder to the hut. As the afternoon wore on, Thunder fought off hunger and thirst. She ran her fingers along every board, probing for openings, but found nothing. Her left foot snagged a sliver, so she sat, and while searching for it, her fingers accidentally brushed over her swollen toes. To her surprise and disappointment, they had no feeling. *They should have begun to heal by now.*

While staying busy at the school had distracted her from the pain of separation from Golden Eagle, it had never waned. Now, all alone in the dark hut, her heart yearned to see him. She remembered how good she had felt before the surrender. Now, the ache of being apart nearly swamped all the wonderful feelings she'd ever had.

To her relief, Miss Graves let her out at sundown.

As instructed, Thunder returned to Miss Ortega and Miss Lorence at the infirmary three days later. Miss Ortega grimaced as she inspected Thunder's two little toes, now black and swollen at their base. "I must remove your two dying toes," she announced, "or a fatal illness may spread throughout your body. If we don't cut them off, they will poison your body as they die, and that might kill you."

Flushing with rage, Thunder glared at Miss Ortega. *Miss Lynch caused this, and you did not stop her!* Immediately, she regretted her harsh thought. Miss Ortega had no more power to stop Miss Lynch than she did. Calmly, Thunder looked back into Miss Ortega's sympathetic eyes and pondered her situation. She consoled herself. *This will only affect my damaged leg.* Remembering stories of people running without small toes reassured her. Thus, she dismissed the loss and decided to face the amputation as a warrior. "Cut them off now."

"I have something to deaden the pain for you."

"I don't need it."

Miss Ortega looked surprised. "Well, all right."

Miss Ortega went into another room and brought back an armful of items. "I was worried when I last saw your toes. I had the fort's blacksmith make simple tools so the amputation will be as quick and accurate as possible." She placed wound dressings, two pieces of metal, and a hatchet on a low table. From under the bed, she pulled out a small, low bench with a block of wood on top. She turned to Thunder. "Now slide over to the middle of the bed, so you only need to lie back after the procedure."

Thunder did so, and Miss Ortega knelt, lifted her leg, and placed her foot on the block. She took out some awful-smelling fluids, and Thunder felt her wash thoroughly around her bad toes. She tried to wiggle her toes for the last time. *Empty the mind and let my warrior spirit carry me through the pain.*

Miss Ortega raised the hatchet and brought it down. As Thunder heard the *thunk* of the hatchet, a searing pain tore up her leg. She swallowed the pain and stayed silent. Miss Lorence grabbed the bandages and covered the wound, while Miss Ortega turned Thunder and eased her back on the bed. She raised Thunder's foot and slid folded blankets beneath it. "This will help stop the bleeding."

Thunder lay still, bringing her mind to the source of the pain
—*Miss Lynch*. Her thoughts went unbidden to Golden Eagle, Grandfather, and Young Falcon. *Restraining my rage against Miss Lynch*
will not be easy, but I will try.

～

Suns turned to moons, and the moons turned to seasons as time at the
school crawled slowly on.

After Thunder's scuffle with Miss Lynch, two armed soldiers
stayed in one of the small buildings, within calling distance of the
teachers.

Thunder never forgave Miss Lynch and avoided her; Miss Lynch
seemed to return the favor. Fortunately, the food had improved. The
people in the eating room provided bread and meat daily, and fruits
and vegetables in season. Rumor spread that they had a new, less
corrupt agent who did not steal the most valuable provisions.

As Thunder had once adjusted to Chiricahua life, she now
learned to live among the whites. She worked hard at ciphering
numbers and reading and writing English. Whenever beyond the
teachers' earshot, she asked Helen to translate into Spanish any
phrases she had heard throughout the day. Gradually, she mastered
much of the white-eyes' language.

From time to time, Thunder came across some of the younger
girls. They longed to return home, but they were healthy and treated
well. Thunder had learned that Miss Ortega, though under Miss
Lynch, was the head teacher for the younger students.

Thunder, too, was homesick. She often wondered what had
happened to Stormy, imagined Young Falcon happy with her new
baby, and thought of Golden Eagle and Grandfather several times a
day. With the love for her people burning brightly in her chest,

Thunder learned to follow the rules—or rather, learned to avoid getting caught breaking them. She grew accustomed to the school routine, and she even enjoyed learning, especially English.

Miss Graves and the other teachers constantly reminded the class of how much they loved the students. The teachers' actions, completely at odds with their words, puzzled Thunder. *Why do you punish the people you love?* The pain they inflicted taught her to hate their beliefs, not embrace them.

On Sundays, the teachers required all the students to attend service in the large church. Thunder enjoyed the silence and beauty inside the building with its vast space, high ceiling, and whitewashed walls. But she found Miss Graves' sermons absurd and boring.

Miss Graves told the students her people's God loved all Indians. This new word, *Indian*, surprised Thunder. The word grouped the Chiricahuas with the Mescalero Apaches, the Navajo, the Hopi, and all the other tribes known to her, into one people. She realized she and the girls from other tribes did indeed have much in common. Their peoples all lived in small groups, using what nature provided. They asked the spirits to reveal their wishes, and all lived by wisdom superior to the white-eyes.

The schoolgirls were also told all native people were heathens. Thunder did not know what that word meant, but Miss Graves made it sound very unsatisfactory. She explained Indian gods were pagan and Indian beliefs barbaric. All the teachers maintained only one true God existed—a white one! If Thunder did not accept him as her savior, he would condemn her to burn forever in a place called Hell.

Thunder had never heard such a ridiculous story. All Apaches knew when the life force left the body, a person's spirit was transported to the underworld. If a person was killed unjustly, the death must be avenged before the soul could be set free. And that was that.

Miss Graves said God was jealous, and anyone who worshiped

another would suffer severely. In fact, the teacher had a whole list of things they were not allowed to do. Anyone who did not heed this list would go to the burning place after dying.

Those souls who had lived correctly would go to Heaven, the white God's city of gold in the sky. Thunder pondered this, unable to understand how God had made a whole village of gold. Every Apache considered the yellow stone too soft to make things with, so they made their jewelry and other objects from silver. The Apaches knew of many mountains filled with the yellow stone, but they considered these mountains sacred, belonging to Ussen. No Apache would touch gold.

One Sunday, Thunder asked Miss Graves if her God had stolen the yellow stone from Ussen's sacred mountains. Miss Graves furiously ranted that her God, the only God, did not steal. She sent Thunder to the woodpile to chop wood for the rest of the day.

As Thunder worked, she pondered, *I am an Apache, and they want me to become something else. Their punishments will not change me. I will never be like them.*

Thunder listened to their prattle for many moons, but she never believed it. She did not know why the teachers professed this madness, but she did know questioning it enraged them. So, silently and alone, she promised she would always believe in Ussen and hoped Ussen would not be angry if she pretended to believe in the White God. She hoped Ussen was not jealous too. She doubted that, though. Surely Grandfather would have told her.

One morning, Miss Graves told the class that long ago, God had declared a tribe called Jews to be his special people. When they disobeyed him, he became angry and punished them in awful ways. He destroyed their villages with floods and famine, and many died.

The more Thunder learned of the White God, the more he frightened her. She began viewing the church as her adversary and the

White God as a harbinger of death. White people and their God were full of anger, danger, and treachery, so she spoke whatever words they wanted to hear. To survive, she hid behind a mask of smiling and gave the impression that she thought like the teachers. She learned to lie very well.

EIGHT

New Mexico Territory, October 1878

One day during morning classes, Miss Lynch brought a new girl to the room and introduced her as Agnes. Thunder was curious about the hatchet-faced girl with piercing, bright brown eyes—already in braids and a settler's dress.

At recess, away from the teachers, Thunder introduced herself. She quickly learned Agnes belonged to the Mescalero Apache people, who spoke a dialect practically identical to her own.

"I am Three Hills Chiricahua," Thunder said with glee.

Agnes smiled, then frowned. "Did the soldiers destroy your village too?"

"Yes, they forced us to build a new village on their reservation." Thunder paused a moment, then asked, "What is your real name?"

The girl beamed. "Walks Alone." She looked down at her dress.

"I hate this ugly thing. When the soldiers brought me here, they took me into a room with Miss Ortega, then stood outside. She plaited my hair and begged me to change into this dress myself. Miss Ortega told me if I did not comply, the soldiers would put it on me by force." Walks Alone scowled as she tugged on a braid. "If the teachers want me with braids, I want them out."

Seeing Miss Graves approaching, Thunder motioned for silence. "Follow their gestures, answer to Agnes, and do not speak near the teachers. I will find you soon and help you survive this place."

Miss Graves told Thunder to go play with the others. As she walked away, she heard the teacher call for the soldiers. They came and stayed near Miss Graves and Walks Alone for the rest of recess. When the bell sounded, the newcomer stayed put. Miss Graves called, "Agnes!" and pointed to the buildings, as she and the soldiers strode toward the girl. Walks Alone ignored them. When one soldier grabbed her wrist, she struck him with her free hand. The other soldier seized her from behind and they dragged her to the hut.

Thunder found Walks Alone at breakfast the next morning. She stayed near her throughout the day, but the teachers always lingered too close for them to speak. At recess, Walks Alone kept to herself, kicking at the gravel and dirt at the edge of the play yard.

That night, while the other girls slept, Thunder wanted to get to know the newcomer better, so she crept to Walks Alone's bed. Within moments, she learned the girl's Mescalero village was a five-sun's ride to the east of Thunder's home. However, Walks Alone began to cry as she told her none of her people had survived the swift, overpowering attack on her village. As the girls wept quietly together, Walks Alone spoke of seeing her friends and relatives butchered by soldiers. Thunder tried to imagine how her new friend felt. *All my people massacred...how horrible! I cannot stay that deeply in Walks Alone's pain.* Thunder blocked the unbearable thoughts from her mind. Through most of the night, she stayed with Walks Alone in her grief, though she could say nothing to lessen it.

Before Thunder returned to her bed, she tried to persuade Walks Alone to pretend to adjust to school life, as she herself had done. "I have been here ten moons; pretending is the best way to avoid punishments."

Walks Alone sat, her head down, not saying a word. Thunder admired the proud, unrepentant Apache, and it troubled her own conscience. Tallying how much she had given up in order to survive, Thunder grew ashamed of herself. Walks Alone slowly looked up and glared at her as if she beheld a traitor.

The next morning, as Thunder approached the eating room, Helen came through the door and whispered, "Walks Alone wore a stone necklace to breakfast."

"Why did you not stop her?"

"The teachers had already seen her wearing it."

Thunder huffed in exasperation. Expecting the worst, she entered the room and saw Miss Lynch snap the string of stones from Walks Alone's neck. The Mescalero lunged for Miss Lynch, swung both hands to the woman's throat, and squeezed hard. Miss Lynch tried to break free, but she couldn't budge the grip. Other teachers called for the soldiers as they tackled Walks Alone, taking Miss Lynch with them. Eventually, they pried Walks Alone from the coughing, gasping Miss Lynch, and held her down until the soldiers arrived and grabbed her. Miss Graves ordered them to take Agnes to the hut, and they dragged her away.

Assisted by Miss Graves, Miss Lynch climbed to her feet. She turned her back to the students, then bent over and went into a coughing spasm. After standing and raising her hand to her throat, she rolled her head around and hacked some more. Still breathing heavily, she faced the students and straightened her clothes and hair. Her eyes were watery, and her face shone bright red.

"Students," she said in a hoarse, high-pitched voice. She sniffed a few times and cleared her throat. "Your attention, please. All of you are responsible for Agnes' savage behavior. Everyone's food rations will be cut in half until we civilize this animal." She coughed again and walked away.

The girls let out a collective groan as Thunder observed their frowning faces. *Now the whole school is against Walks Alone. I would have stopped her from making that necklace had I known. She must have collected the stones at recess and tied them together with one of the kindling bundle strings.*

The students received half-empty plates for breakfast and for each meal that day. Early the next morning, Thunder and the other girls awoke to Miss Ortega's clapping hands. Beside her stood Walks Alone. Thunder felt everyone's wrath upon the girl in disheveled braids.

"Do I have a volunteer to re-plait Agnes' hair?" the teacher asked.

She sent Walks Alone to her bed, where Thunder quickly joined her. "Are you all right?" she whispered while taking out the braids.

"Yes," the Mescalero said in a hushed tone and looked about. "Miss Lynch ordered I not eat until I answer to Agnes and follow the rules."

Thunder parted the girl's hair down the center of her head. "I can help you do that."

"I have been hungry many times. An empty stomach is not much of a threat."

"You will not last long without food. If you appease the teachers, you will avoid the hut too." Thunder began to braid her left side.

"I am starting to like the hut."

Thunder pulled Walks Alone's hair, twisting her head around. She stared into her eyes, whispering harshly, "We all hate that hut! Why would you like it?"

Walks Alone blinked. "Nobody bothers me. I will not get food anyway."

Miss Ortega gazed at them. Thunder finished the plait with a tie and moved to the right side. "Listen," she whispered, "I detest Miss Lynch as much as you do. I promise to help you get revenge once we are out of here, but now we have no choice; we must bide our time."

"After the whites took everything from me, I would rather die than submit."

The bell clanged, and Thunder hastily knotted the braid tie. As the other girls began preparing for the day, Thunder got off the bed, dumbfounded. *Walks Alone really means it. No time to persuade her now.*

"Get dressed," Miss Ortega said, looking at them sharply.

Thunder nodded and turned her eyes to Walks Alone. "Just stay close to me today, and we will talk soon."

Thunder did not allow Walks Alone out of her sight while getting ready. The other girls grumbled about their empty stomachs and made Walks Alone the target of many dirty looks. But they did not confront her directly, knowing she would thrash whoever dared start a fight with her.

On their way to the eating room, one of Walks Alone's braids had lost its tie and began to unfurl. Thunder had to fetch a replacement before a teacher noticed it. "I need to get you a braid tie," she told Walks Alone. "Save me a seat for breakfast—and do not say or do anything else." Thunder hurried for the dormitory.

Upon returning to the eating room, Thunder saw the soldiers—with Miss Lynch and Miss Graves—all surrounding Walks Alone.

No braids? She must have just taken them out. She should have listened to me...I cannot help her now. One soldier grabbed her right arm and the other her left while Miss Lynch took scissors from her pocket and cut off Walks Alone's hair. Apache girls drew great pride from their long hair and Walks Alone flew into a rage.

Dorothy and her friends stepped closer and chanted, "Filth and lice! Filth and lice!"

"Lock her in the hut," Miss Lynch ordered.

The soldiers slowly dragged Walks Alone away.

Apparently afraid Walks Alone would escape, the teachers had the dormitory windows boarded up and a lock placed on the door. After dark, soldiers were posted outside the room.

Thunder began pocketing much of her food and slipping it to Walks Alone at night. She tried to shield her friend from Dorothy and the other girls, but she could do little about Miss Lynch or the teachers.

The teachers continued to abuse Walks Alone. One day, Thunder could no longer stand it, and she furiously cursed the teachers, demanding they stop. They laughed at her, then Miss Graves took her through the rain to the hut. The roof had many cracks, and the rain poured in. Time seemed to stretch on forever. The rain finally ended and the world went dark. Thunder sat, soaking wet, shivering helplessly until Miss Lorence let her out the next morning.

Walks Alone never said prayers, nor did she answer to the teachers in the classroom. She never picked up a slate tablet or piece of chalk. Not once did she answer to the name Agnes. The teachers made an example of her, punishing her day after day for her defiance. They whipped her with leather straps, slammed her against walls, and forced her to kneel in a corner throughout the day. At night, they shackled her to her bed. Each morning, Miss Graves led her to the classroom on a wide leather leash, tied her to her desk, and watched her as closely as an eagle watches a snake.

Thunder grew angrier every day. Miss Graves warned her not to interfere, ordering her to stay at her desk. Thunder obeyed but seethed and wracked her brain to find a way to end Walks Alone's torment.

One morning, Miss Lynch opened the hut door, and Walks Alone stepped out, looking as thin as a skeleton. Thunder's heart sank when she saw her face, swollen and bruised almost beyond recognition. Her bleeding mouth hung open, revealing broken and missing teeth. But Thunder lost all hope when she looked into the girl's eyes. They were dead. No anger, no fear, nothing.

Thunder continued to share her food, putting her own health in peril. One afternoon, she fainted. She awoke to Miss Ortega's pleasant voice in the infirmary, offering her a plate of food. For three days, the good-natured woman coaxed Thunder into eating more from each plate than she had in weeks, and eventually dismissed her saying, "Eat all your food to stay healthy." Thunder wanted to explain why she had eaten so little, but Miss Ortega seemed to already know.

When Thunder returned to the dormitory, Walks Alone had disappeared. Her inquiries about the girl yielded only frozen stares. Later that night, Helen whispered, "Your first night in the infirmary, Walks Alone tried to escape. They must have caught her and locked her in the hut. On the second morning, we found the hut open. They took the boards off the dormitory windows, put us on regular rations, and we haven't seen Walks Alone since."

Thunder never forgot the hatchet-faced girl and often prayed she had escaped from the hut. A month later, during recess, she crested a hillock and discovered a cemetery. Walking among the grave markers, she found one that read "Agnes."

NINE

New Mexico Territory, February 1879

One morning well into Thunder's second year at the school and her fifteenth winter, Miss Graves sent her to the principal's office. Unaware of the reason for the summons, Thunder feared she would be punished for some unknown offense.

Principal Smith's sympathetic smile caught her completely off guard. "Your grandfather is very ill. He has requested your return to the reservation."

Ill? Concern for Grandfather flashed through Thunder's mind. She had not seen him for so long. *I must return to him at once. But how?*

"I see here on your last teacher's report," the principal continued, "that you have mastered the basics of ciphering numbers. More importantly, it shows your ability to read and write English is outstanding; because of your academic progress, I am going to grant his petition." She picked up papers from her desk and looked them over. "Your grandfather also mentioned that other people are sick and some babies have died. Since the younger girls from your village have similarly done well, I am allowing all of you a one-week visit to the reservation."

Thunder politely thanked the principal and returned to her room to gather her few personal belongings.

On the long ride to the reservation, she wished instead she were going home—to her real home in the mountains. There, everyone had been happy and lived with abundance. She remembered Principal Smith reading the message Grandfather had sent. *Has he grown more ill since he sent it? Could Young Falcon's child be among the dead? Golden Eagle could also be among those suffering. Stormy: what has become of him?*

Thunder cleared her mind of worry and turned her thoughts to the week before. Miss Graves had taken ill for three days, so Miss Lorence had replaced her.

The new teacher had not followed the lesson plan. Instead, she had told the class much about the white people's world that they had never seen. She spoke proudly of trains that carried many things at high speed, and the telegraph that sent messages far distances in moments. She also talked of many cities; villages so big, it would take nearly a day to walk around one.

Maybe the whites like such things, Thunder had mused, *but my people have no use for them. We are happiest in our land with belongings of our own making.*

For the rest of the day, Thunder thought about the oddities of the whites, making her wonder about her fight with Polecat, and Snow separating them. The next morning, just as Miss Lorence began class, Thunder raised her hand and asked, "Why would a soldier stop an Indian and another soldier from a bare-handed fight?"

The teacher thought for a moment. Her demeanor changed as if she had recalled something. "If either had died, the soldier would be responsible and would need to tell the reasons to his superiors. They would expect him to have done everything possible to stop the violence. If he did not, they would put him in a prison cell for many months or years."

"What is a prison cell?"

"It's like the punishment hut, but it's usually a big building divided into small rooms with enough space for those punished to lie down. They are provided water and simple food." Miss Lorence looked at Thunder knowingly. "Harriet, see me after class."

Thunder worried she had asked something wrong. When the bell clanged, she waited for the other students to leave before approaching the teacher.

Miss Lorence finished erasing the blackboard, then turned and said, "I've heard something of the situation surrounding your arrival at the school. You were very lucky that soldier found you and intervened in the first place. Few other white men would have risked their lives for your safety." She smiled. "You are dismissed."

Thunder left the classroom, trying to piece things together. *My people would never punish an onlooker for the actions of two people settling a grudge.* Remembering the misery of staying in the hut for even a day or two, she cringed at the possibility of causing Snow years of suffering. *I will find a way to express my gratitude to him, whether he knows of it or not.*

Upon arriving at the reservation, the younger girls went straight to their families while Thunder made her way to Grandfather's lodge. He sat outside the wikiup—chipping on a long piece of flint—and looked up, his hair grayer and his face more wrinkled than she expected. She ran to him as he got to his feet and greeted her warmly. Remembering his poor health, she embraced him gently. She released her hold, and said softly, "Dear Grandfather, I am so happy to see you again." But she saw no signs of illness. "The principal told me you were sick."

"First, step in out of the cold, Daughter," he said as he held the flap open to let her enter.

Inside, Thunder lit a small fire, and both settled in.

"I and others pretended to be ill in order to have all of you returned," Grandfather said with a smile, then sobered. "We all must escape within a few suns. When the new agent arrived a half-moon ago, our provisions trickled down to nearly nothing."

"Is that why the babies are dying?"

"Yes." Something about her caught Grandfather's eye. "Has your ear been injured?"

"Nicked by a bullet a long time ago," she said flatly. "Much has happened since then." Recalling she wore a settler's dress, Thunder looked through the Apache clothes she left behind and found her beaded bracelet and dress. Grandfather's expression turned solemn as he watched her. He seemed eager to know more but remained silent.

She hastily slipped off the settler's dress, donned her old buckskin garment, and retied her bracelet. Both fit more snugly than when she had last worn them. This surprised her since she had not eaten well at the school. Grateful those days had ended for now, she stood a little straighter, feeling victorious and empowered. She was still an Apache; try as they might, they had not taken that away.

"I have something for you," Grandfather said. He extended his open hand to Thunder. In it rested a small pendant of sandstone, carved in the shape of the thunderbird.

Thunder accepted the pendant gratefully and tied it around her neck. "It is beautiful," she said, caressing the stone with her fingertips. "I am sorry I have nothing to give you, Grandfather. I was not allowed to make any Apache things at the school."

"I assumed so," Grandfather said softly.

After a pause, she asked, "Has Golden Eagle come back to the reservation?"

Grandfather sighed. "We have waited for the soldiers to return all the braves before we try to escape. Now the fort is almost finished, so nearly all the young warriors have been brought back, and I sent for you. Only Golden Eagle, Two Feathers, and Crossing Wolf still work there, and we do not know when they will return. We must escape without them."

Thunder's deep disappointment must have shown on her face since Grandfather abruptly asked her about her experiences at the school.

Thunder talked about the friends she had made and her classes in arithmetic and English. Delighted to speak in her native language, Thunder told stories far into the night. She took care not to speak of any cruelties, choosing to share her troubles another time. Grandfather praised her greatly for having learned the language of the white-eyes.

Later, she lay awake reflecting on being back home. Despite the awful news, she was so happy to be among her people. *How can I leave Grandfather again?* As she thought about it, her aching heart turned into a physical pain that settled in her stomach. It began churning and cramping until she had the strong urge to vomit. *I cannot return to school. It would tear my heart from my chest to abandon my people again.*

The next morning, Thunder stood outside and watched the snow fall aimlessly. The cold wind caused her to shiver and pull her robe tighter around her body. She walked around the reservation and observed for herself what Grandfather had told her. Over a hundred of her people, all thin and hungry. Seeing Young Falcon and her son, Little Bird, gaunt and malnourished made Thunder's soul ache. *The people must have food, but I would hate to leave without Golden Eagle.*

She returned to the lodge. "Grandfather, we will lose many if we try to escape now. If you can speak to the new agent and get more provisions, we will not need to flee, at least for a while."

Grandfather hesitated. After a long silence, he said, "Yes, you may be right. But I do not trust their translators. We should speak to him together."

"I will go with you."

"Good." Grandfather smiled. "We will try your plan first. But during your absence"—he pulled an unfinished flint spearhead from his pocket with a devilish expression on his face—"we secretly made bows, arrows, lances, and clubs. If the agent refuses to help us, we will use them to fight our way to freedom."

At the agency office, soldiers told Thunder the new agency master, Mr. Blomgren, wished to speak to the entire tribe. Thunder translated for Grandfather, and they returned and spread the word among the people.

Soon afterward, everyone gathered outside the agency office. With Thunder translating, Gray Fox tried to explain the poor living conditions were severely affecting the Apaches' health; in particular, the children suffered. Thunder realized how difficult it was for him to plead and to suppress his pride for the good of his people.

"There is only one way I'll increase your food allotment!" the agent shouted. "You must tell me where Geronimo's camp is!"

"*Gokliya?*" Gray Fox wondered. "I have been here many moons. How could I know where he is camped? Even if I did, I would not tell you. We are *Hiuhah*, men of the rising sun. We have lived by our wits for hundreds of years. Do you really expect me to sacrifice our great warrior chief for the comfort of my kinsmen?"

Thunder considered whether to literally translate her grandfather's harsh words, wondering how Mr. Blomgren would react. She decided to forge ahead word for word, proud of Grandfather for standing up to the white-eyes' leader.

Blomgren's face grew purple with rage. He turned to the guards and yelled, "Lock him up!" Looking back at Thunder, he added, "Tell him there will be no more food until I know where Geronimo is hiding!" Thunder paled as she repeated the captain's order. He had gone too far.

As the guards hauled Gray Fox away, the Apaches faced Blomgren with hard, unyielding stares of bitter resolve. It soon became obvious the Apaches would divulge no information, so Blomgren ordered them back to their lodges and stationed two sentries near their village. Using horsewhips, the soldiers lashed anyone who walked too slowly.

That night, it turned bitterly cold and began to snow. Thunder had seen heavy snow in the mountains, but never such large flakes as now fell on the reservation. The next morning, a blanket of snow covered the land.

At mid-afternoon, Grandfather returned from the stockade. Purplish-black bruises covered his swollen face, and his nose, once long and straight, curled like an eagle's beak. Thunder felt ashamed. *I asked Grandfather to speak with the agent because of my selfish wish to wait for Golden Eagle. Not only have I caused*

Grandfather to suffer, I have made it more difficult for him to lead our escape.

A crowd of angry Apaches quickly gathered, but before anyone spoke, Gray Fox held up his hand and said softly, "We should wait until late at night to speak when most of the soldiers are sleeping."

"We owe our *nantan* this much respect," Soaring Hawk affirmed. No one denied Gray Fox's request.

Later, after the cold had driven most of the guards indoors, Gray Fox gathered his people around a campfire. Thunder saw an unquenchable thirst for revenge in her grandfather's eyes and heard the same in the warriors' voices.

"Let us escape now!" Blood Moon announced. "I am going out there to kill as many as I can!"

"I am with you," Horse Walker agreed. "It is better to die quickly than to watch our children starve."

Gray Fox gestured for silence. "We agreed to stay under the rule of the white men until we replenished our weapons," he said firmly. "Now we have plenty of weapons but no food. In a few suns, we will be too weak to use the weapons to escape. I agree with Blood Moon. If we must die, then let us not die in captivity like cowards. Let us die the true Apache way—fighting!"

Muted cheers, kept low so as not to alert the guards, rumbled around the campfire.

Gray Fox continued in a soft voice, "We will hide in the small cavern on the other side of the woods. The entrance is overgrown by brush, so the white-eyes will have a hard time finding us. Go there as fast as you can. The warriors will hold back any soldiers trying to stop us. Horse Walker, Too Tall, and Skilled Roper will take out the night guards."

The Apaches hurriedly painted their faces black with ashes from the edge of the fire. The warriors retrieved weapons from their lodges, and men, women, and children silently slipped from the village, taking only what they could carry on their backs.

As Grandfather had requested, Thunder was seeing everyone safely underway, when a shot rang out. An ugly wave of disappointment welled from within her. *Our plan is ruined. Bluecoats will be upon us any moment.* She took the last bow, strapped a quiver full of arrows onto her back, and hurried to find Grandfather. Somewhere behind, she heard running feet that could only be soldiers in pursuit.

The snow had now become their enemy. To the Apaches' misfortune, a full moon shining on the pristine snow turned night almost as bright as day. Thunder heard gunshots and bullets whizzing alarmingly close to her. As bodies dropped in the snow, she frantically looked around for Grandfather. Some people had fallen behind, while others not burdened with children had pushed forward. *Why is our escape so disorderly? The people seem directionless.*

The warriors let loose a flurry of arrows from behind the cover of rocks and trees. Many soldiers fell, as others moved back. Thunder did not see Grandfather among the warriors. *Where is he?* She wanted to help them fight, but she had to find their leader.

Seeing footprints leading toward the cavern caused Thunder's hopes to soar. She continued running and prayed to find him among those survivors.

Amidst the clustered people, she finally located Grandfather, without his bow, kneeling against a big pine tree. His hands clutched his chest as he gasped for breath. He looked all around, blinking as if greatly confused. She froze for a moment in shock and pity. *He is unable to fend for himself, much less lead. No wonder we are in such chaos.*

Thunder started toward him but had to stop when she stumbled over a soft mound in the snow. Looking down, she saw a cradleboard, and next to it, Leaping Fawn. The young woman lay in the snow, blood pumping from a bullet hole in the front of her dress.

"Take my son," she pleaded.

Thunder reached down to help her.

"No, save my son—it is too late for me." She reached feebly for the cradleboard.

Judging from the amount of blood in the snow, Thunder agreed. A bullet hissed past and smacked into a tree, causing her to jump. She picked up the cradleboard, slipped it on her back, and ran toward Grandfather.

Arriving at the old man's side, Thunder wedged her bow between her back and the cradleboard, then took his arm. "We must go, Grandfather."

She pulled him up, and he leaned heavily against her as they stumbled onward through the pine trees. *Why is Grandfather unable to keep his balance? Is he injured?* Lifting his left wrist, she ducked under his arm to take his weight. After they ascended a hill, she stood gulping in cold air, thanking the spirits for the baby's silence. Though pain still pierced her lungs, she knew they had precious little time to rest. Grandfather was weakening. *If I do not find shelter soon, he will die. Please, Child of the Water, help us find refuge nearby. We will never make it to the cavern.*

The soldiers closed in again as Thunder helped Grandfather across the rocky hilltop. Gray Fox seemed befuddled. She had never seen him so vulnerable.

"I can hardly move my leg," Grandfather mumbled. With a groan, his knees buckled, and they both fell to the ground. Thunder knelt and felt his leg for any broken bones, protrusions, or blood. *Nothing.* She sat him up, squatted, and ducked under his arm again. "Grandfather!" she implored. "Get up, please. You are sacrificing yourself!" She took his wrist and tried to stand.

"Take pity on an old man. Leave me here to rest," he whispered, his voice weak as a child's.

"We will be shot if we do not leave now!"

Bullets sang past them as she lifted Grandfather to his feet and lugged him toward the edge of a cliff.

As they made their way down a steep pathway along the bluff, she said, "The snow is changing into rain. It is very slippery, and you must be careful."

"I will try," were all the words his wheezing chest would allow.

Guiding him carefully over slick stone, Thunder saw what appeared to be a small cave ahead. Grandfather silently rubbed his head, as if afflicted by pain. Something was wrong. Terribly, terribly wrong. Thunder talked to him as though he were a child. Her gentleness seemed to calm him as she continued leading him downward. It seemed his spirit had departed, leaving only an empty shell. Somewhere deep inside, she knew without him, her people would all perish.

Approaching the cave, she was grateful to Child of the Water for the hiding place. She silently gave thanks for the cleansing rain, which would wash their footprints from the snow.

Once safely inside, she helped Grandfather lay down. She patted the old man's hand to reassure him of her love. She set the cradleboard on the stone floor and tenderly reached into the blanket. To her shock, the baby was cold. When the blanket fell from his lifeless face, waves of guilt washed over her. She recalled the baby had not cried or moved since she took him from Leaping Fawn. He had been dead the whole time. The hollowness in her chest grew unbearable as she tucked the blanket back around him. Now, she could only wait for the light of morning to prepare his soul for the underworld. Exhausted, she lay down next to Grandfather. *I can only hope he is better in the morning.*

Thunder awoke to a gray sky above the western horizon, her body stiff and sore after a night of little sleep on the cold stone floor. A thick strip of moonlight illumined the cave. Grief swelled in her heart as she scooped out a cavity in the loose rocks and gently placed the cradleboard into the shallow hole.

"Grandfather," she rasped, then took a ragged breath. "The life force of the small one has departed, and we must send his spirit on his journey."

The *nantan* sat up and looked through half-lidded eyes at the dead baby. "You did all you could, Daughter. Do not sorrow for the child's passing. Instead, rejoice, for his soul has been set free."

Thunder noticed Grandfather's left arm oddly hugging his chest. *That is not good. Best not ask him about it.* Instead, she sent up a prayer of thanks that Gray Fox's mind had returned.

She weighed his words and wondered, *Is it only in death we find freedom?*

By the time Thunder finished readying the child's final resting place, a bluish glow had appeared on the horizon. "I must see if we can leave now," she said. "The soldiers will find us in the light of day."

Gray Fox sat looking at the dead infant, pondering his own brush with death the night before. The numbness of his left leg and arm had rendered him unable to walk without Thunder's help. Even worse, he could barely see when Thunder aided him to the cave. He shut each eyelid, testing his vision. His left eye saw nothing. He rubbed his cramping arm and struggled to his feet, then shuffled around the cave trying to limber up his stiff knee. As the *nantan*, he had to press onward for the sake of his people. Steeling himself for the journey ahead, he took a deep breath and prayed to the spirits for the strength and clarity to lead his people to safety. He would be content with the granting of this lone wish.

Thinking of Thunder's skill and persistence of bringing him to safety, he realized what a competent warrior she had become. He raised his arms to the heavens as best he could. "Ussen," he called softly in the stillness, "protect this girl, for the Chiricahua will need her strength to survive."

Then, in a quiet voice, he sang the baby's soul into the next life.

TEN

New Mexico Territory, February 1879

Soon after sunrise, Thunder and Gray Fox entered the brush-covered cavern beyond the woods and found the rest of the survivors. To Thunder's relief, Young Falcon, her son Little Bird, and Soaring Hawk had all escaped unharmed. But she was devastated that more than half of her people had died trying to get away. Sunflower had treated the six wounded. They were weak but could still walk, though three needed aid to travel. One hundred and five escapees had dwindled to fifty—nine younger than twelve winters. The blood of the fifty-five lost souls would leave the land red for many, many moons.

Gray Fox had chosen their refuge wisely—the cavern had a small exit at the far end. Despite his limp and curled arm, he hurried everyone out of the exit and away from the soldiers. Thunder's heart ached at the sight of his suffering. "Can I help you, Grandfather?"

He smiled. "Do not fret, Daughter. I am fine."

She walked on, discreetly wiping away tears, wondering whether the escape was worth such a huge loss. *Over half of us dead. For what purpose? We were starving and tried to reason with the agent. What else could we do? Everyone agreed to leave.* She thought of Firemaker and Silver Leaf and all the other brave warriors who had lain down their lives for others. *I now hate the whites as much as Walks Alone.*

Toward the day's end, Gray Fox's people made camp in a narrow valley lined by gigantic oak and hickory. The fifty survivors camped in rocky terrain, not as a strategy, but simply because they could go no farther. They were a motley band: wives with no husbands, husbands with no wives, parents with no children, and children with no parents.

Taking her bow and arrows, Thunder left the camp in search of game. An angry wind gusted snow across the valley, bowing the heads of the younger trees. *Testing,* she thought. *Something or someone always tests our strength.* The trees looked naked and forlorn against the barren landscape. The fierce howling of starving wolves made her wonder whether they were being tested too.

Later, as the daylight faded, she found a meadow but saw no wildlife. She dismally considered turning back empty-handed. However, a movement among the pines sparked her curiosity. Approaching, she found three horses, far past their prime, nibbling on clumps of tall grass protruding through the snow. *Good in their time, but now too weak to work a full day, and not of much use to anyone.* Thunder smiled. *Except us.* She watched the mare and two geldings move as they ate. *Mangy and all their ribs showing...but none are limping. Probably abandoned by settlers or frontiersmen.* Despite their age and scrawniness, she decided to take them back to camp.

Mindful of the growing darkness, she pulled up a yellowish clump of grass by the roots and approached a chestnut gelding. Once he began to nibble, Thunder knew she had a friend. She gave him long, caressing pets down his neck and along his body. When he nuzzled against her, she wrapped her arms around his neck and swung herself up onto his back. She easily rounded up the other horses, and they loped across the snowy meadow to camp. *These horses are livelier than I thought,* she mused.

The Apaches, sitting huddled together along the base of a huge granite cliff, cried out in elation when they saw the horses. Blood Moon raised his bow and drew a bead on the weak old mare.

Thunder looked at her former instructor in dismay. The tribe would chastise her if she stopped him from killing the horse for meat. Then, it dawned on her. She was still worried about the disapproval of others, as she had learned at the school. *I need to speak truth, like an Apache, not lie like a white-eyes for approval. Yet I hate to confront my teacher who helped me learn to run again.* She dismounted, stepped into Blood Moon's line of fire, and said in a firm voice, "We need all three horses to flee from the Bluecoats."

"My wife, all my children, and grandchildren were killed during our escape!" Blood Moon shouted. "Now we are weak from hunger and have no food. Who are you to say I cannot make meat for all of us from an old horse?"

"We can live without meat another night," Thunder countered, sure Blood Moon would relent after considering a plea from one of his most ardent students. "I am sorry about your family, but every one of these horses will help save us from meeting their fate."

The older people looked at Gray Fox, who stood close to the fire, kneading his curled fingers. Thunder was sure what they were think-ing: Gray Fox was the *nantan*, not this sharp-tongued granddaughter of his.

The old man finally looked up. "I believe Thunder is right. We will need every horse. The scouts can ride them out to find our way, or they can carry our most gravely wounded."

Already dusk, the people—resigning themselves to another night without food—settled around the campfire. Thunder squeezed in among them, ignoring a few critical looks. No one spoke. Grandfa-ther had taught her long ago Apaches treasured silence. It calmed one's mind, opening it to the wisdom from the spirits.

It was the time when day was almost over and night had not yet begun. It was the time when day creatures grew quiet and moonlight animals had not yet found their voices. It was a time when all you have lost weighs most heavily on your mind.

A distant coyote began singing its lonesome song. Thunder listened to its voice as it rang among the other spirits of the night. The lingering golden-orange glow of the fire seemed to push back the blackness of the canyon walls. She studied the flames' small fingers as they reached out toward her people's gaunt faces, exposing their stony, pain-filled expressions. The night seemed endless. The moon appeared, crossed the sky, and started its decline. Still, no one spoke.

They had set up this hasty camp and started a fire among some boulders to hide the firelight from enemies, hoping the stones would also break the ever-blowing wind. The wind had not obliged. It remained relentless, hammering the cold against the suffering Apaches.

Thunder awoke from a half-sleep as sunlight crept its way across the land, the morning air blue with cold. Blood Moon, the night guard, had let the fire go out. Thunder watched him sleeping at his post. *Some protector. If the soldiers had come, they would have attacked without warning. His family's deaths have seriously affected him. He taught me better than that. We cannot trust him now.*

Although she had wrapped her hands in rags to keep her fingers nimble, they were still stiff from the cold. Reaching for her water-skin, she found its contents frozen solid. She gathered deadfall and upon returning, she noticed Sunflower dabbing the horses' open-sored spots with salve. Once the new fire burned briskly, the people came to warm themselves.

Gray Fox walked up to the fire, his left arm hugging his side. He looked soberly at his followers. "My friends, we have no time for mourning in the old way," he said with regret. "We cannot help the poor souls left behind, but in their honor, we must fight to survive and raise our children."

"How can we fight against guns with arrows?" Blood Moon challenged.

Anger darkened Gray Fox's eyes, briefly before his expression softened. "I am sorry you lost your entire family during our escape, but we can do nothing about it now." After taking a deep breath, he said in a confident voice, "We are too few to stand alone. Our strength will multiply if we are bound together. It is the Apache way. We must think and act as one, stay together, and share what we have."

Looking around at his people, Gray Fox asked, "Will someone lend me a blanket?" Sunflower pulled her worn robe from her shoulders and handed it to the *nantan,* who spread it on the ground. "Let all who agree put their possessions on this blanket. Soaring Hawk will have the responsibility of distributing the goods. Those who wish not to share should take what they have and go. But leave knowing you are cast out—you may never return to this band."

Blood Moon stood. "Without family, I have no reason to stay."

He looked around and strode to the mare, mounted, and then rode off, his bow and quiver swaying on his back. Thunder fought to suppress her anger; she wanted to stop him. *He should be allowed his weapon, but he has no right to take the horse. A mentor to whom I gave great respect is beyond reconciliation. Though it tortures me, it is best to let him go.*

Grandfather remained silent, giving others a fair chance to depart. To Thunder's relief, no one followed Blood Moon.

Running Coyote came first, laying his rabbit skin on the blanket. Rolling Cloud followed and put down her mother's cooking knife. Thunder smiled, glad to see the white-eyes had not changed the girl who helped her thwart Polecat's plan. Young Falcon came next, then Thunder stepped up and placed her bow and arrows among the community's possessions. One by one, every man, woman, and child with belongings added them to the pile.

After the last person contributed, Soaring Hawk redistributed the weapons among the best warriors. He stored the other goods in packs and returned the blanket to Sunflower. "I will protect your belongings with my life," he declared to the people, then turned to Gray Fox and asked, "Will we go to Willow Creek, as you suggested last winter?"

"Yes. We should go now. We can search for food along the way."

After mounting the two worst injured onto the horses, the band of forty-nine began the journey to their new home.

ELEVEN

Sangre de Cristo Mountains
New Mexico Territory, March 1879

One full moon had passed since Gray Fox guided his people to Willow Creek. Everyone survived the transition, and they worked together to establish their new village. The warriors killed many buffalo from a small herd, providing meat and hides for the people. This allowed them to make a few tipis to survive the colder weather and stronger winds in the high mountains. Some people decorated the tipis with brightly colored paintings and drawings. The buffalo and other game also provided cooking utensils and clothes.

As the first day of spring dawned, white frost covered the land, and weirdly shaped ice formations clung to everything. By midmorning, however, the frost had disappeared, and the sun shone brightly.

Thunder helped Young Falcon place Little Bird in his cradle-

board, and they left the village to search for edible plants downstream. "Although I miss our homeland," Young Falcon said as she
looked at the surroundings, "life here is good, away from the reservation and the soldiers." She seemed so happy and carefree. Her
lively eyes shone, and the ivory beads at the ends of her braids
caught the sunlight as she moved. Thunder listened quietly, thinking
how fortunate Young Falcon was to have Soaring Hawk at her side.
The ever-present danger of the Bluecoats made Thunder worry she
might be kept from finding such happiness for herself.

When they reached the warmer lower ground, the women parted
and began scouring for food.

Soon afterward, Young Falcon called to Thunder, and when she
arrived, they began harvesting a patch of yucca plants near a small
cave.

"These new sprouts of yucca will be perfect for our evening
meal," Thunder remarked.

As they gathered the tender shoots, Young Falcon said, "We have
food and a safe place to live now, but you do not laugh with me. It is
not like you to be so quiet."

Thunder cut off a yucca shoot, put it in the basket, and sighed.
"Two things weigh on my mind. First is Grandfather. We can all see
his stiff arm and his limp, but his mind is suffering as well."

Young Falcon nodded sympathetically. "I have noticed that too."

"He still works hard with his good arm and can still fight with
spears, lances, and rock slings. But sometimes his spirit seems to
drift from us."

Young Falcon cut off more yucca shoots. "The mind and body do
not always travel on the same path. But I have seen some return to
themselves in time."

Thunder smiled. "If anyone can recover, Grandfather can." She stayed busy harvesting for some moments. "And there is Golden Eagle. He is still held by the soldiers at the fort."

"The night before we surrendered, I heard a rumor you two were alone away from camp."

Thunder laughed, then grew silent again. She looked at Young Falcon. "We were planning to be married."

"Oh, Thunder, it is such a pity you two are not together." She frowned, her brown eyes showing compassion. "I know Golden Eagle was taken away soon after we arrived at the reservation. You have not spoken to him since?"

Thunder shook her head. "It was impossible, yet my heart tells me he still loves me."

"Perhaps he and his two friends will finish their work at the fort soon. Maybe then the soldiers will set them free, like the other braves."

"Yes, but even if they do that, the soldiers will stop them from leaving the reservation, as they did to us. I am always thinking about Golden Eagle, and my soul aches. The pain will not go away until we are together again."

"I cannot even imagine how I would feel if Soaring Hawk was taken from me," Young Falcon said. "I will pray that the spirits grant your wish."

Thunder rose early the next morning to see a light blanket of new snow covering the land. At the edge of the plateau, a few trees blocked the otherwise magnificent view of the valley. As she walked down the bank to collect firewood, she looked to the side. *The slope looks like a bear claw reaching into the stream.* She slipped on a snow-covered rock and nearly fell. From then on, she watched her every step until she arrived at the creekbank. Reaching for a log, she glanced downstream and shuddered. *Bluecoats!* She sprinted for cover until her foot caught on a hidden vine. Her arms flew up as her body pitched forward, and she landed face down in the snow. Ignoring the pain in her hands and knees, she rose and raced along the stream.

Eyes darting back and forth, Thunder searched desperately for a place to hide in the desolate terrain. With the clamor of hooves already near, she dove into a patch of tall winter grass, narrowly escaping view of the charging soldiers.

They must have somehow killed our night guards. Through the stems and leaves, she saw the Bluecoats holding a rifle in one hand and reins in the other. They swiftly ascended the plateau and headed toward the village.

Soon came the repetitive cracks of gunfire and the high-pitched screams of the dying, each cry piercing her heart. Recalling Grandfather's dictum, *always stay alert for soldiers,* she chastised herself for not scanning the countryside on her way down to the creek. *Those few moments might have been enough to turn back and warn my people.*

The creek's shallow water rippled soundlessly over its rocky bottom, less than a hundred paces below the ridge where her people fought for their lives. Smoke rose over the ridge, and her spirit sank. *The Bluecoats have set fire to my village!*

Grandfather's advice echoed in her mind: *"If we are separated, Daughter, remember: to survive, you must become one with your surroundings."* She burrowed deeper into the sweet-smelling grass, then wrapped her arms around her cramping legs and pulled herself into a tight ball. Her soul was in turmoil. With her training, she belonged up there in the village, fighting alongside her brother warriors. But having no horse or gun she would certainly die uselessly. *I am not scared to fight, but someone must stay unharmed to tend the wounded.* Despite these thoughts, in the darkest corner of her heart, she knew she was afraid.

Sounds of the frenzied attack continued. Trying to quell her trembling, Thunder imagined her grandfather taking aim and throwing a spear. It flew straight into a soldier's chest, the impact killing the man before he hit the ground. Taking another spear, Grandfather searched with his keen eye for the next target. Thunder was so lost in her make-believe world, it took her a few moments to realize the battle sounds had diminished into a heavy, oppressive silence.

When she heard the first muffled footfalls, she lowered her ear to the ground. Listening intently, she recognized the unmistakable flinty sound of horseshoes grating against stone. She parted the thick stalks of grass and watched the soldiers ride down the slope. As the Bluecoats drew closer, she heard them chattering and laughing. With all the commotion, she could only discern a few of their words, but those struck terror. The battle had ended, the soldiers triumphant.

Scarcely daring to breathe, Thunder watched the soldiers reload their guns. Hearing them laughing and talking so nonchalantly enraged her. Apparently, they had no fear of retaliation from her people. Her eyes scanned the hillside. Surely, she would see Grinning Bear and his warriors come swooping down. But nothing moved save the snow-covered mesquites shuddering in the frigid wind.

"Mount up, you bastards. The party's over!" the stocky sergeant barked, digging his heels into soft flanks. His voice was familiar. Thunder noticed the man's eye: it did not open more than halfway.

Polecat! His mare galloped away, but not before Thunder spotted a pair of braids with ivory beads dangling from his saddlebags. *Young Falcon!* Her arms grew limp, and her breath came in short half-gasps, like the panting of a dog. She tried to rise, but her knees buckled and she blacked out.

When she awoke, the mid-morning sun was barely visible through heavy, low-hanging clouds. The cold, damp air chilled her bones and consumed her with foreboding. Ash sifted around her like black rain and the acrid smoke parched her throat, making it difficult to breathe.

Thirst finally forced her from her cocoon of safety. Stifling a cough, she scooted down the crumbling bank to the creek. There, she drank handfuls of icy water to soothe her burning throat. Getting to her feet proved more difficult. Woozy from the reeking fumes that cursed the air, she yearned to crawl back into hiding yet dared not shirk her responsibility to tend the dead and wounded.

Thunder's moccasins crunched lightly on the snow as she climbed the craggy hillside. Fear of what was above became a heavy burden, causing her back to bend and her feet to slow. Every few steps, she stopped to listen, but the stillness only alarmed her more. Even so, nothing could have prepared her for the grisly scene at the top of the ridge.

Thunder stood transfixed by the atrocity. The melting snow was red with blood, more blood than she had ever seen. She watched tiny red rivulets cut through the glistening white crust to gather into puddles and congeal in the late morning sun.

Moving as if in a trance, Thunder gazed at the smoldering piles of debris, remembering how beautiful the camp had looked with the sun gleaming on the lodges. The smell of singed hide from the tipis sickened her. Each lodge had stood so proudly, its painted symbols depicting the history and heroic deeds of its family. *Gone,* her spirit murmured. *Every lodge, every memory, gone.*

The silence of the death site was impenetrable, dark, and unholy. Nothing could be heard, not the call of a bird or even the wind whispering through far-off trees. It was a silence that seemed to echo the soldiers' taunting laughter.

A chilling breeze swept across the camp, carrying most of the remaining smoke with it. Heartbroken, Thunder surveyed the destruction, unable to fully register the sight of her people strewn haphazardly like children's buckskin dolls. To her right lay the twisted body of Grinning Bear, his muscular arms trapped beneath him, still clutching his lance in readiness to fight. Grinning Bear would fight no more. His bowels lay spilled upon the ground.

Thunder swung away from the appalling sight, only to stumble over Sunflower. A trickle of blood still dripped from her slit throat. Why had the soldiers needed to kill this wise, compassionate old woman?

Thunder lifted her head to the sky. "Why?" she asked the spirits. "Why are my people so hated?"

She turned and saw Soaring Hawk and his warriors scattered everywhere. Death had altered the familiar faces, changing them into strange, grim masks. Warriors always gathered together in order to draw enemy fire, giving the women and children time to escape. Heavily outnumbered, the Apaches had been no match for the repeating rifles of these enemies.

Thunder's heart pounded like a drum. The stench of charred flesh filled her nostrils, and she fell on her battered knees, retching repeatedly. When the spasms passed, she rose, oblivious to the slush now puddling at her feet. She wiped her face with snow, hoping the cold would restore her ability to think. She forced herself to count the bodies and added the two lost guards: all but one of the villagers, dead.

Numbed by shock, she refused to acknowledge the carnage before her was family and friends. A glimpse of a worn buffalo robe, some distance from the others, tore her mind from its retreat. A malignant fear threatened to steal her sanity as she ran across the battlefield and fell upon a shaggy heap lying in the mud.

"Grandfather!" she wailed.

Turning his corpse over, Thunder was shocked to see the vacant eyes of her beloved grandfather staring back at her. Her fingers frantically pulled aside the buffalo robe and exposed his deerskin shirt, riddled with bullet holes. The bead and quillwork she had so carefully created had been ripped away. "Another white-eyes' souvenir," she whispered bitterly.

Drained of all strength, Thunder sagged forward and fell upon her grandfather's lifeless body. She buried her face in his robe and smelled its stale odor of tobacco, sweet now with the memories of the old man she had loved so dearly. For the first time in her life, she felt alone, utterly alone.

Cradled against her grandfather, she rocked back and forth, wailing. Tears fell, and she let them stream freely. Surely the spirits would not punish her for this weakness. When at last her weeping subsided, Thunder felt exhausted, yet somewhat relieved of the terrible grief inside of her. She snuggled deeper into the pungent robe, almost hearing her grandfather say in his raspy voice, *"Breathe deeply, Daughter. Hold the air in your lungs for a moment, then exhale slowly."*

Following his instructions, Thunder breathed, continuing the exercise until she relaxed. She touched her grandfather's face tenderly, tracing each worry line that life's struggles had forged.

Lifting her voice to the wind spirits, she thanked them for granting her the privilege of being his granddaughter.

Thunder rose. A ferocious anger began to boil in her chest, and scalding tears gushed down her wind-chapped face.

"Aiieeeeeeeeeeee!" The piercing death keen surged from her lips. Her white-knuckled fist shot into the air defiantly. "White-eyes will die by this hand!" she swore in a shrill, inhuman voice. "For I, Talks Like Thunder, have spoken!"

TWELVE

New Mexico Territory, March 1879

As the sun traveled midway toward its rest in the western sky, a blustery wind buffeted the desolate field of death, rousing Thunder to her senses. She wished to stay resting at Grandfather's comforting side and not face the harsh finality of burying him. Despite her protest, however, she had to find a proper place to send Grandfather's soul to the spirit world.

She remembered the small cave, near the creek, where she and Young Falcon had found the yucca plants. It was not big enough to fully protect and hide Grandfather's corpse, but she knew of no other possibility. *It will have to do,* she thought with resignation. She needed a pole drag to move his heavy body. It would please Grandfather, though, to rest among the rocks in the cave. He had always said only good spirits dwelled among stone.

Two poles from a smoldering lodge caught Thunder's eye as suitable for a pole drag. She separated the thin logs from the stinking ruin and dropped their fiery ends into a puddle to extinguish them.

Thunder needed supplies in order to survive. Working her way around the village, she carefully sifted through what remained. She could not find cooking tools or weapons. The soldiers had burned almost everything, and even the two old horses lay dead. At the edge of the smoldering fire, she found a shoulder pack and some burnt-off lengths of rope. After few steps, she came upon a waterskin she could use as a canteen, as well as a buffalo-paunch, both miraculously undamaged.

"Thank you, teacher," Thunder said politely while removing a bone-handled skinning knife from the hidden pocket in Grinning Bear's knee moccasins. "I will remember all that you taught me." Apaches never accepted a gift without returning one of equal or greater value. It pained her to give away the thunderbird pendant Grandfather had given her, but it was the only gift she had. She slowly raised it over her head and placed it around Grinning Bear's wrist. "May this help you on your journey to the underworld."

As she shambled through the devastation, Thunder tried not to look at the corpses. But unbidden, her eyes locked on Young Falcon, lying face up on the ground, her scalp missing, her skull crushed. Her arms still reached toward her unfortunate toddler. The sight triggered a new roiling in the pit of Thunder's stomach. She turned quickly away but could not obliterate the sight of Little Bird's chest, run through by a white-eyes' bayonet. She shuddered violently, picturing Young Falcon's long braids swinging from the sergeant's saddle.

"May your brains burst, you white-eyed sons of the devil," she shrieked, "and may your blood pour across Apache land!" She picked up the dead toddler and laid him next to his mother. Consumed with fury, she raged and cursed the soldiers.

The lodge poles had cooled when Thunder returned. Laying them side by side, she bound them together with willow branches to make a pole drag. She turned Grandfather onto his side, set the drag next to the corpse, and rolled him onto it. Needing something to erase her tracks, she spotted a cedar tree, cut off a branch, and placed it on the drag beside him.

Straining her body, her moccasins slipping against the damp sandy soil, she pulled Grandfather toward the cave. Winded after a hundred paces, she went back and removed her tracks. Each round of pulling and sweeping became shorter until she still lacked air when re-yoking to the drag.

Muscles aching, she again lugged the drag forward. A new upward slope of the land demanded more of her strength. *Am I trapped in an endless horrific delusion?* Oblivious to veering off the trail, her mind seeped into a dreamworld. *Arms full of firewood, back at the village, people preparing the morning meal, everything as expected—*

Thump! Her foot hit a rock, and she toppled over it. Gasping for breath, she rose. In her exhaustion, the world began to spin. Leaning into the harness to keep her balance, she pulled ahead. The whirling landscape had lost its color, each step less than a moccasin length. Her burden seemed immovable. *Nothing will stop me from bringing Grandfather to his final resting place!* Amid the churning surroundings, she caught sight of the cave and locked on her goal.

Finally, she reached her destination, dropped the drag, and took several moments to regain her breath. Using the last of her waning strength, she lifted and tugged, until she finally heaved Grandfather onto the small ledge of the cave. Unable to combat her exhaustion and uncaring of her hunger, Thunder lay down in the cave beside him to rest. As the daylight faded, the gods of sleep soon whisked her spirit away.

In the darkness, Thunder awoke screaming, nightmare visions of the massacre replaying behind her closed eyes. She thrust her thumbs against her eyelids and pushed. Dazzlingly bright lights filled her vision amid a pain that dimmed the vivid agony of her people's fate. "I should have been up there fighting with the warriors," she lamented. "Then I would be dead like everyone else."

Praying to White Painted Woman, the virgin goddess who gave life to the Apaches, Thunder asked for strength to carry out her duties the next day. Lonely and frightened, she again lay down beside her grandfather for the emotional security his cold body provided. Apaches feared people once the life force had left them, but she could never fear Grandfather or even his ghost. She snuggled closer.

After a night of sporadic sleep, Thunder awoke at sunrise. Tenderly, she reached for Grandfather's robe and tucked it around him. Touching his cold, unyielding flesh brought back the previous day like a slap across her face. Tears threatened. Sinking her teeth into her lower lip, she resolutely kept them at bay.

Never would Talks Like Thunder forget that day. Never would she forget the odor of burnt flesh. Never would she forget the faces of the little children whose bodies lay smoldering beneath the silent gray skies. Never would she forgive Polecat for killing and scalping Young Falcon. Like a true blood Apache, she would walk the path of vengeance until all the souls of her village were set free!

She knew death held many mysteries. Grandfather had said that when someone died, the ghost of a loved one guided that person's spirit to the underworld which was comprised of two lands: a green valley for virtuous people, and a barren dwelling for evil ghosts and witches. Thunder knew the burial liturgy must be observed correctly, or a spirit might become stranded among the living. If allowed to wander, such a ghost might cause sickness or even death.

She thus followed the rituals as best she knew. The thought of her mother came to her mind. Thunder hoped she had reached her spiritual home among the virtuous.

Thunder fetched water from the creek, and gathered sage, red ocher, and dried moss for the burial ceremony. After bathing Grandfather, she carefully painted his face with the ocher to symbolize the return of his body to the earth. Thunder stared at the old man. *When did this great chief become so frail? The years on the reservation had been hard on everyone, especially the children and the old ones.*

At mid-morning, Thunder wrapped Grandfather in his buffalo robe and placed him to face the setting sun. *His spirit can choose from several possible paths after death. He might reincarnate as a different human being, an animal, or travel to his soul's original home, the "Other World."* She wished she could give him his weapons and personal belongings to ensure his spirit a safe, comfortable journey. Unfortunately, all had been lost except his tobacco pouch and the medicine amulet hanging from his neck. She did not touch the amulet, knowing it contained Grandfather's sacred powers, but she removed the tobacco. She would need it later.

Making a small fire of the moss, Thunder fed the tiny flame with dry sage leaves. She stroked the fragrant, sacred smoke over Grandfather with his eagle feather. After purifying him, she returned it to his plump braid.

She set aside the ashes and carried rocks, one by one, to cover Grandfather's final resting place. Thunder preferred that wolves or coyotes not feed on Grandfather's body, but she understood the never-ending cycle of life. She did fear, however, that white-eyes might return to scalp and mutilate the body. Such a sacrilege would prevent Grandfather's spirit from entering the land of peace and love. It would trap his spirit among the heartless invaders.

Halfway through her task, she sat by the entrance of the cave.

Relieved from her labors, she reflected on all she had lost. *First my father, then my mother, then my best friend, my beloved Grandfather, my entire village…*

She rubbed her bracelet, contemplating the deaths of her loved ones. The people of the Chiricahua village had now joined the White Mountain Apaches of her childhood, vanishing from her life. She renewed her promise to always wear the bracelet, in memory of all she had lost.

The loud cawing of a vulture transported Thunder back to her task. *I need to cover Grandfather completely.* She labored on and on until mid-afternoon. While placing the last stone on her grandfather's tomb, she heard his wings of spirit flutter away. Thunder sighed, relieved to know Grandfather's spirit was now soaring on its way to the underworld. She gave a pinch of tobacco to each of the four sacred directions and chanted a final prayer, asking the Ganhs, the mountain spirits, to watch over her grandfather on his journey.

She paused for only a moment before grasping a handful of her hair in one hand and Grinning Bear's bone-handled knife in the other. With a flurry of hacks, she severed her long, silken hair. She then slashed at her arms, swinging the knife in a frenzy until blood dripped from her fingertips. Thus, she mutilated herself, the customary way of showing one's grief. Cutting off an arm, though, would not have been enough to express her feelings of sorrow.

Later, Thunder returned to the base of the tomb, and sat cross-legged. She smeared her face black with the ritual ashes and sang the ancient mourning song. The mystic, age-old murmurs reminded her of how she felt while walking in a forest or on a mountaintop. The high-pitched keening of her death song echoed softly along the hills, then died like her family and friends. Loneliness stabbed her with a physical pain. She clutched her chest as though to stop her heart from breaking. *How will I live without Grandfather and my people?*

From the darkness of despair, a ray of hope came to her mind: a glimmering pair of smoke-gray eyes. *Golden Eagle, thank the spirits that you could not escape with us. You may still be in captivity, miserable, cold, and hungry—but at least you are alive.*

Continue Thunder's journey. Scan the code below to dive into book two: *Falling Star*.

Turn the pages to read the first chapters of *Falling Star*.

FALLING STAR

Far from one-year-old Desert Flower, then living in the White Mountains, something happened in a millisecond on the Great Northern Plains. An ancient soul returned to earth from the spirit world to serve the Cheyenne people by planting the seed for a tribal rebirth.

ONE

Dakota Territory
(Present-day Wyoming), July 1865

The village was quiet. Children, adults, and old ones sat by the communal fire, sipping tea after the evening meal. Father Sun had gone to rest, and murky clouds blocked most of Moon Maiden's reddish-orange light as she slowly rose above the horizon.

"Look, everyone, look at the sky!" Red Flower screeched. All eyes followed her gnarled finger to an eerie cluster of dark clouds above them.

The full moon appeared through an opening in the eastern clouds, most of it blotted out, only a remnant shining. The world bathed in unearthly light. An unexpected chill embraced the village, a vicious wind whipping across the scorched earth.

"Death stalks our village this night!" another woman wailed, as a coyote howled from somewhere in the nearby mountains, informing the shaman that evil spirits were loose in the night.

Great streaks of lightning veined the sky and a clap of thunder jarred the earth. Rain spattered in huge drops, blending into a solid wall of water. Villagers ran in haste for shelter. Abruptly, the rain stopped and the moon turned an ugly, dark blood red.

"The storm gods have eaten the Moon Maiden!" came a distressed cry from the darkness.

"Quiet, old woman," Red Flower grumbled, "or they will eat us too."

Suddenly, for one breathtaking moment, a star arced its way down toward the earth, blazing with pure white light. The star exploded, radiating a blinding flash. The stunned villagers stood speechless, looking at one another in bewilderment.

From the birthing tipi, the cry of the shaman, Raven's Wing, shattered the silence and resounded throughout the village. The Cheyenne people, renowned for their bravery, now cringed in fear, waiting for death's blow by some demonic hand.

After some time, Long Bow and his Dog Soldiers, their weapons ready, cautiously crept toward the tipi. The coyote's warning had made them anxious to learn Raven's Wing's fate. When the warriors rounded the tattered lodge, their eyes widened in surprise, for at the entrance stood their shaman.

Raven's Wing, the most esteemed holy man in the Cheyenne nation, stood calmly rocking a newborn baby. The long tendrils of his yellowish-gray hair glowed, and the dark circles under his sunken eyes made him appear ghoulish. The awe-stricken warriors stared at the shaman as if he were an apparition from the spirit world.

Finally, Long Bow regained his senses and stepped closer. "Grandfather! We thought the demons had come for you!"

"No, my son, I have seen no demons. I cried in joy when I saw this miracle birth. My vision has come true!"

The frightened women and children still expected the worst as they crept behind the Dog Soldiers.

"Sound the drum," Raven's Wing directed. "We must call the tribe to council."

Raven's Wing's pronouncement spread through the village like a windswept fire. Moments later, the heavy thuds of the drum summoned everyone to congregate at the middle of camp. Chaos ensued as the adults sat, jostling for their favorite positions in a circle enclosing the central clearing. Everyone talked at once with no regard for customary courtesy.

"What do you suppose has happened?" Lame Leg asked.

"I do not care to guess," Spring Clover said, shrugging her bony shoulders.

"The end is coming," Red Flower declared. "The end is near."

Astonished, the women turned to Red Flower. "Why do you say that, Mother?" Lame Leg asked, even more curious than before.

"Too long we have had to run from the Wasichus, who are taking our land. Though we know our prophet Sweet Medicine warned us against following the invaders' ways, drinking their firewater alone has made us foolish. The Great Spirit has been offended, and now comes the day of reckoning. Now comes the time for our punishment."

Red Flower's words stunned the people into silence as they hunched over and crossed their arms. Their fear of the presence of spirits caused them to stay on guard for something to happen.

At last, the aged shaman appeared, looking mysterious with his face painted in black and white polka dots. He stepped through a gap in the circle of seated Cheyenne and emerged into the vacant center. Like an ancient oak, Raven's Wing represented a timeless strength.

Although his fringed leggings hung loosely about his frame, their bead and feather ornaments cast a sense of elegance. His sunken chest was bare, save the yellow orb painted to resemble the sun.

A spine-tingling hush fell upon the crowd when the old man lifted his arms to the sky. The gourd rattles in his bird-like hands came alive to tell an ancient story, his worn moccasins moving gracefully to the rhythm.

The primal throbbing of unseen drums joined in, causing each heart to quicken. When the tempo reached the proper pace, the warriors joined Raven's Wing inside the holy circle. They began a summoning dance to invite the spirits of their ancestral fathers to this sacred meeting.

Raven's Wing lowered his arms, and the drumming stopped. Most of the warriors seated themselves with the people in the outer circle. Some, however, remained in the sacred area, where they stood in a new, smaller ring. The old man took his position of honor in this circle of the council. He sat cross-legged, and the others seated themselves according to their stations.

When everyone settled, Raven's Wing opened the pyramid-shaped bag of soft white deerskin and took out his long-stemmed red clay pipe. He methodically lit it and drew in smoke. The first puff he blew up toward the sky, saying, "To the home of all spirits." The second went downward. "To Mother Earth." The following puffs went to the four sacred directions:

> West, to the land of thunder spirits who give us rain.
> North, to the spirits who send us great cleansing
>   winds.
> East, to the spirits of light who give men wisdom.
> South, to the spirits of summer who hold the power to
>   grow all living things.

All these spirits are forever aspects of Maheo,
the Great Spirit, the All-Knowing One Above.

Raven's Wing passed the pipe to the warrior on his right, who did not smoke from it but handed it on to the next man. Thus, the warriors passed the pipe around the circle, unsmoked, in the direction opposite the sun's course. Upon its return to Raven's Wing, he blew smoke from the pipe and gave it to the man on his left, following the course of the sun. Each man took his turn, believing the ascending smoke to be his own breath carrying his words to the Great Spirit.

When the ritual was complete, Raven's Wing set the pipe aside to cool before returning it to his bag. He slowly rose and began to speak, despite murmurs in the crowd. "I have called the ancients to this council to verify the miracle we have witnessed here tonight. They are here to guard my tongue so no untruth shall be spoken.

"Many years ago," Raven's Wing began in his best story-telling voice, "the Great Spirit sent the prophet Sweet Medicine to teach and guide his Cheyenne children. Before Sweet Medicine died, he predicted what would come to pass in later years, including our present time. For you young ones who may not know his revelation, I will give you the gift of his wisdom."

The children and adults fell silent and turned toward Raven's Wing.

"'One day,' Sweet Medicine proclaimed, 'the time will come when you must fight, for each tribe will want the land of another. My children, you will be driven from your land and earthen lodges. You will no longer know the tranquility of life as growers but will be forced off the land and out of your dwellings. For the Cheyenne nation to survive, you must become hunters and warriors. You will be nomads and find refuge in the west, on the Great Plains. You will live in skin-covered lodges, eating the meat of a great shaggy-haired beast. With the passing of many seasons, there will come a strange animal. It will have round hooves and teeth on the top as well as the bottom of its mouth. It will have long hair growing from its neck and a hairy tail that almost drags on the ground. You must not eat this animal but learn to ride upon its back. For when the shaggy beasts grow fewer, you will have these 'long tails' to help you hunt for elk and deer.

"'When the shaggy beasts are no more, there will come a smaller animal with short hair. Some will have spots of color on their hides. The meat will not be as sweet and succulent as the shaggy one; none-theless, you must learn to eat it, or our people, the Tsetsehesestahase, will die.'"

The crowd stayed silent, and their eyes widened.

"'During this time, there will be many changes in your lives. Strange men will come from a faraway land. Their skin will be white, and many will have eyes the color of the sky. Some will have hair growing on their faces. These men will eventually rule the land. You will follow the ways of these white men and become worse than crazy.'"

Raven's Wing sank slowly to the ground, his frail body quaking from exhaustion. He was very old, so old that even the next-oldest member of the band could not remember a time when he was not already an old man. Although he had earned the respect of every chief in the Cheyenne nation, here he was more than respected—here he was loved. Many times, he had proven himself a great healer and advisor. The fact he had lived so many years was proof enough he communed with the spirits.

The Cheyenne people waited for their shaman to regain his breath.

Seeing the people face him and begin to whisper, Raven's Wing seized the chance to reclaim their rapt attention. Silence fell as he rose, took a long draught from his waterskin, and began to speak again.

"We know the words of Sweet Medicine are true!" He paused to be sure all were once again listening. "Just as he predicted, our ancient fathers were forced from their native land of the Five Great Lakes. We have indeed become hunters and warriors who roam the plains. We also live in tipis, ride horses, and hunt the disappearing buffalo. We are exactly as he proclaimed we would be.

"If we cannot go back to our traditional ways, the rest of the prophecy will come to pass. We will live on the white man's reservations, where they will strip our way of life from us. Is this not the worst fate? To lose everything we hold dear?"

Raven's Wing paused to let these truths touch each heart. "We have watched the sky-eyed strangers take our land and kill our buffalo. We can do nothing, for they are countless. Like blades of grass on the prairie, for every one we kill, ten more appear. They have already forced our sister tribe, the Southern Cheyenne, to move far south to a reservation alien to us. I do not wish to go where so many have gone and never returned. The buffalo are our food, clothing, lodging, even our tools and weapons. Without them, our people cannot live as the ancients did. As Sweet Medicine foretold, we must learn to eat the meat of these strangers' 'cattle.'"

A powerful spirit seemed to fill Raven's Wing. "The words of Sweet Medicine," he declared, "no longer hold hope for us. Another leader, another prophet, must speak to us and intercede with the spirits, that the Cheyenne may yet live under their guidance. That leader has come to us now!"

Drawing a deep breath into his shallow lungs, he gave the people another moment to absorb the truth of his words. He continued. "Many moons ago, a spirit came to me in the night, saying, 'Watch the sky, my son. You will know when the new leader is among you, for I shall light the path to earth with a star.'"

Raven's Wing gestured to Fears No One, the baby's father. He rose, cradling a blanket-swathed infant in his arms, and approached the shaman.

"Tonight, my brothers and sisters," Raven's Wing intoned, "when Moon Maiden hid her lovely face in darkness, I witnessed a star plummeting to the earth. At that exact moment, this child came howling through the tunnel of life!"

As Raven's Wing took the infant from the blanket, he gazed into the newborn's black, glimmering eyes, seeing a light, a depth of soul, that confirmed his intuition. In his arms, he held a messenger from the Other World.

He turned and lifted the squirming baby toward the crowd. "Here is our new leader!" he proudly proclaimed.

TWO

Dakota Territory
(present-day Wyoming), July 1865

"It's a girl," someone whispered.

The young warriors stared at one another, confused. However, most of the tribal elders, including war chief Long Bow, believed the phenomena proved the girl was their shaman. Certainly, Raven's Wing's endorsement answered any further doubts. Raven's Wing ended the meeting and tenderly gave the infant back to Fears No One.

As the women and children left the grounds, the younger men jeered, refusing to even consider obeying the demands of a girl. Glares and upheld fists showed their discontent.

Raven's Wing was disquieted by their rowdiness, but it didn't surprise him.

Through the early night, warriors discussed the ramifications the newborn would have for the tribe.

"We will be laughed at if we take orders from a girl," Buffalo Bull lamented.

"We will obey only powerful men," Broken Lance confirmed. "That is the way it has always been, and the way it will always be."

The warriors rushed to stand beside Broken Lance, wanting to show how many fighting men the tribe would lose if the elders persisted with this nonsense. Cheyenne men were tall and agile. They were hardy warriors and skilled hunters and held many competitive war games to keep themselves in prime mental and physical condition. To take orders from a girl was unthinkable!

The women, having fewer formal societies, later convened a meeting to discuss Raven's Wing's surprising revelation. They crowded into a large tipi on the outskirts of camp and seated themselves inside. Mother Hawk, Chief Elk Horn's wife, rapped her walking stick solidly against a big drum to quiet the chattering women. "I have called everyone here because of the baby girl who Raven's Wing believes will be our new leader. Many of the men stand against her and may keep her from maturing into a shaman. My first question to all of you," Mother Hawk said slowly as she looked pointedly around the lodge. "How many of you believe the girl born tonight is destined to become our new leader?"

Hous of affirmation resounded throughout the lodge.

Taken aback by such an enthusiastic response, Mother Hawk rapped on the drum again. "Come to order, ladies, please." She then tried the opposite approach. "Does anyone think we should *not* accept this child as our new leader?"

The entire lodge became silent. Mother Hawk called out, "This is your last chance!" No one made a sound. "Then, it is unanimous. We agree to accept her as successor to Raven's Wing."

Hous resounded throughout the lodge again. The Women's Society had never before agreed unanimously on any issue; this was an extraordinary event.

Mother Hawk hammered on the drum many times more before regaining control of the meeting. When the women quieted, she lowered her voice to a near whisper. "Since we all agree this girl will someday be our shaman, we will encourage her whenever she behaves in unusually holy or knowledgeable ways. We will teach her to see, act, and think as a shaman is normal and expected. For her sake, we must subtly and carefully do this around the men."

"Then, we should inform our husbands, should we not?" Lame Leg asked.

"For the love of spirits, no!" Red Flower yelled, even before Mother Hawk could answer.

"No," Mother Hawk concurred, "we must not tell our husbands, or the men will think we are trying to control them. Our choice to stand with the girl as our next shaman needs to go to our graves with us. Does everyone agree?"

Again, *hous* carried the motion. The women joined hands and swore an oath of secrecy.

Raven's Wing held fast to his convictions. It did not matter to him that the child was a girl. Intuitively, he knew she was destined to be the Cheyenne's next great shaman.

Although Snowbird and Fears No One disliked this intrusion into their personal lives, they honored the tribe's welfare above their own wishes. They made no objection when the old shaman named their child "Falling Star."

As the moons passed, the controversy over Falling Star's future leadership continued, but no one could deny her exceptional nature. She radiated a feeling of an ancient soul, elevated beyond the cares and concerns of ordinary people. As word of the fulfillment of Raven's Wing's prophecy spread throughout the Cheyenne nation, the women in every band supported her appointment.

Cheyenne women were among the most attractive of Plains Indian women and Falling Star's unique beauty surpassed all expectations. Her small, heart-shaped face displayed perfectly chiseled features, and her dark brown eyes shone brightly with intelligence.

Raven's Wing observed how the child bonded with her surroundings without fear of anyone or anything. His visions revealed she had not come to live a conventional life with the Cheyenne people, but rather to serve them. In the years to come, the Great Spirit would lead her to a far northern land to fulfill her destiny.

~

Continue Thunder and Star's journeys. Scan the code to read book two: *Falling Star*.

Marjorie Carter was born in Salem, Missouri, on July 17, 1937. Of Cherokee descent, she learned the traditional ways of her relatives from early childhood. During the eight grade, she was forced to leave school to work and provide for her younger brothers. At the age of nineteen, she moved to Texas and began her careers in the restaurant and real estate businesses. During her life, she was diagnosed with seven different cancers and fought against melanoma for 25 years. A Native American seer and shaman, she had a passion for art, poetry, and stories. She wrote at her ranch near San Miguel de Allende, Mexico, hoping that Red With Native Blood would help reservation students embrace their heritage. Marjorie died of pneumonia on July 12, 2004.

Randal Nerhus received a BS in Agricultural Studies from Iowa State University in 1982, and an MA in Oriental Philosophy and Religion from Bananas Hindu University, India, in 1988. Shortly after obtaining his agricultural degree, he volunteered with the Peace Corps in the Philippines. While traveling in the mountains on the island of Palawan, he visited a remote tribal village and encountered a very different way of life—one of community, contentment, happiness, and love. Fifteen years later, his interest in tribal traditions deepened while taking part in a ManKind Project initiation that used native approaches to bring men into a life of integrity. In 2002, Marjorie Carter took him under her shamanic guidance which complemented and expanded on his early Christian foundations. From 2013 to 2016, he lived in Colombia's Amazon jungle studying under Cocama shaman don Rogelio Carihuasari, and relevant parts of that experience were incorporated into the trilogy.

Learn more about the *Red With Native Blood* series, as well as news and events at:

Randalnerhus.com

Facebook: Randal Nerhus-Red With Native Blood

@RandalNerhus on Twitter

RandalNerhus on Instagram

Randal Nerhus on LinkedIn

Randal Nerhus on TikTok

Printed in Great Britain
by Amazon